We dedicate this book to Elizabeth and William, Ida and John, and their descendants.

Elizabeth Carlson has a journalism background and a Fine Arts Diploma in Creative Writing. For over 20 years, she maintained a working relationship with several B.C. West Kootenay newspapers. Her freelance writing has appeared in a number of general interest magazines including publications for seniors and children. Short stories were included in three anthologies. Her most recent published novel was *Anna's Story* (2021). Elizabeth lives in Chilliwack B.C., has three daughters, eight grandchildren, and five great-grandsons.

Janice Lochbaum, co-author, is a retired registered nurse with a Masters in Science. While having a strong interest in writing since she was a child, most of her professional writing experience has been with health research papers, and project proposals in legal and health areas while working in senior health care positions in B.C. More recently, she has been assisting her mother, Elizabeth, with writing, fact-finding, editing, and researching/documenting of family history. Janice is married and lives in Chilliwack, B.C., and has three sons and two grandsons.

Elizabeth Carlson and Janice Lochbaum

LILY'S JOURNEY

AUSTIN MACAULEY PUBLISHERS™

LONDON ● CAMBRIDGE ● NEW YORK ● SHARJAH

Ordering Information
Quantity sales: Special discounts are available on quantity purchases by corporations, associations, and others. For details, contact the publisher at the address below.

Publisher's Cataloging-in-Publication data
Carlson, Elizabeth and Lochbaum, Janice
Lily's Journey

ISBN 9798886939330 (Paperback)
ISBN 9798886939347 (ePub e-book)

Library of Congress Control Number: 2023920926

www.austinmacauley.com/us

First Published 2024
Austin Macauley Publishers LLC
40 Wall Street, 33rd Floor, Suite 3302
New York, NY 10005
USA

mail-usa@austinmacauley.com
+1 (646) 5125767

Elizabeth and Janice are thankful for the support and encouragement of their family, especially Jill, Jo-Anne, Janet, and Becky, who are all Lily's direct descendants.

Part 1

When Elizabeth looked for the first time at the tiny infant in her arms, she said to the nurse standing beside the bed, "She's as perfect as a lily."

With a tightening of her lips, the woman said in a straightforward way, "You must be prepared, Ma'am. She may not make it. I've weighed her and she's just over three lbs."

Elizabeth straightened in the bed. "Of course, she'll survive! Look at the way she balls her little fists. She's a fighter. And ready to take on the world."

The nurse did not respond. She plumped up Elizabeth's pillows. "The master has been pacing back and forth like one of his hounds, Ma'am. Shall I invite him in?"

"Please do."

William hurried into the bedroom all smiles. He bent and kissed Elizabeth. "Well done, my dear." He peered at the baby wrapped in a lacy shawl. "Not much to her, about the size of one of Lolly's pups." Tentatively, he touched the baby's forehead. "And you, Bessie? You are well?"

"Right as rain. I'll be up and about before you know it. I see you're dressed to go out?"

"I'm off to the garden to tend to Lion. Silly bugger found a bunch of thistles." Lion was the hound that lived on the premises of the family's walled garden situated two miles from their townhouse.

Elizabeth indicated the nurse to lay the baby in the crib beside the bed. "It's a little early for vegetables, but see what you can find, Will. There might be a few carrots left from last year."

Before leaving, Will approached the crib. He looked over his shoulder at Elizabeth. "Have you thought of a name?"

"Lily, like the perfect flower she is."

He nodded. "Good enough."

The following day, brother George visited Elizabeth. She had insisted on getting out of bed into a chair that overlooked the side garden. She also had insisted on discarding her nightgown, replacing it with soft undergarments and a robe. A little earlier, she had given baby Lily a small amount of diluted milk, and the infant had taken about half. Earlier, she had decided not to nurse. Throughout the night, Elizabeth had ensured the infant was breathing. And several times had adjusted the crib cover over the tiny form. As much as she told the nurse that Lily would live, she was not totally convinced. The next three days would tell the truth.

George, like most men, was not comfortable in a room with anyone ailing, especially a room where recently someone had given birth. But Elizabeth saw he was doing his best. He was smiling as he approached her chair, leaning over to kiss her on the cheek. "It was good news from the messenger, Bessie. I haven't come empty-handed, I dropped off flowers with your housekeeper. Had to get them from the greenhouse at this time of year. I didn't see that husband of yours about. Expect he's celebrating."

"William was in earlier. He's gone to the shop because they're shorthanded."

"I see. Well, so this is the new arrival." He bent over Lily's crib. "Tiny little thing," he said.

"Yes, but well cared for, babies grow fast, and so will she."

"I expect so." George and his wife, Sophie, had no children.

"Have you picked a name for her?"

"Lily, like the flower. You'll recall I have them growing in the front garden."

"Ah, yes, but I do believe she needs more of a handle. What about Sarah Lilianna? Sarah, after your dear mother, and Lilianna after your aunt."

Sarah, after giving birth to twelve children, nine still living, passed away three years after Elizabeth was born. The only memory Elizabeth had of her mother was when she descended the stairs, she ran her hand down the banister to make sure the maid had dusted. Recollections of her father, Albert, who died a few years after Sarah, were vague, but the brothers kept the parents alive with small stories.

Elizabeth's older brothers also remembered their grandparents, relating small tales about them, like the one about Granny Eliza, who was kind to the gypsies who camped in the lower field while picking fruit on the farm. Granny found a baby girl beside the road. She wrapped the infant in a blanket and took her to the lower field, handed her to the first person she met. "She belongs here, and make sure she stays," she said in her matter-of-fact way.

Albert was also loved by the gypsies. The hearse that carried his body to the cemetery drove along a road lined with daisies, and stalks of buttercups laid there by the gypsies to show their respect.

Now years later following the birth of baby, Lily, Elizabeth watched George prepare to leave the bedroom.

"I'll give the names you suggest some thought, George," she said.

"Good enough. I presume that husband of yours won't forget to register the birth at the County office; he ought to be able to leave the shop long enough for that."

"Be assured he'll take care of it."

George stood by the open door. "I'm going up to London tomorrow to talk to your brother, Alan, about our spring orders. I'll make sure to tell him about the new arrival."

Alan, and his two brothers, Charles, and Wallace, lived in London, managing the Covent Garden's establishment, which consisted of a large warehouse and several offices. Elizabeth rarely saw her brothers. She stayed closer to home, managing the family hotel in the town of Evesham.

The Grande Hotel had been owned and managed by the Albert Dane family for nearly fifty years. Several of the children, including Elizabeth, were born in the upper rooms of the hotel where the family lived. According to old records that dated back to the 1700s, ancestors of the d'Dane family came from France's orchard area. No one knew exactly where, but for the two brothers who left the area, it provided a solid background in market gardening, and farming in

England. The one brother, Charles, did not adapt well to the new country, and returned to France, but his unmarried brother decided to stay in Evesham.

This was Elizabeth's lineage. The next time the surname appeared in records, the 'd' from d'Dane had been dropped, or perhaps lost in recording. Then in 1841 the name appears again with the marriage of Albert Dane, age 26, to Elizabeth Bromley, age 21. From then on census showed each child born to the couple, and the four children who had died at birth.

After Albert passed away at the middle age of fifty-three, son, George hired an estate consultant to manage the hotel, and they, in turn, hired a local man to run things daily. Over the years, there had been many problems with this arrangement. This prompted George to ask Elizabeth, when she turned twenty-five, to take over the management of the hotel. All the brothers agreed.

George and Elizabeth were sitting in high-back chairs in the hotel foyer. A small table before them held a tray, tea pot and two empty cups and saucers. George carefully set the table to the side, and drew a notepad from his breast pocket. Getting right to the point, he said, "You're trained for hotel work, Elizabeth. I want you to take over managing the hotel. I've not been happy with the way it's been run. This way we keep everything within the family. I won't interfere, only make a few changes at the start."

When she hesitated, he said, "It's unlikely you'll marry."

She frowned, not pleased at George assuming she would remain a spinster, but she held her tongue. She was used to George and all the brothers controlling her life.

As if reading her mind, George said, "I don't say it's impossible that you'll find a man that you agree with, but unlikely." She was attractive, taller than most women and had an abundance of auburn hair, usually worn in a chignon. On this day she wore an ankle-length black skirt, long sleeved white tailored blouse with a pearl brooch at the neck. Pinned to the sleeve of her jacket that lay across her lap was a tiny gold watch received on her twenty-first birthday.

After George left, Elizabeth strolled through the hotel, noting the new plumbing on the second and third floors. She proceeded to the kitchen at the rear of the timbered building. This was not her favorite room, although she knew the value of good food served correctly. Leaving the kitchen after a brief look at the spotless counters, she carried on to the sunroom located off the dining room. It opened onto the garden, a favorite place for hotel guests, as well as herself. Only a few blooms remained on this mid-September day. She brushed leaves from a bench and sat down.

She had no choice in agreeing to manage the hotel, and knew within hours, even without hearing back from her, George would notify all the brothers of the new arrangement. She loved him, but there were times when she resented his assumptions. It was true she had been raised for hotel work, helping since she was sixteen, apart from a few months in France with her cousins following school days.

On this day, the hotel was closed to complete the installation of the new plumbing. Her mind was already moving ahead to other small improvements she'd make…

On Elizabeth's 30th birthday dinner, after five years of successfully managing the hotel, she announced she had purchased an eight-room townhouse at the upper end of High Street. Since Elizabeth had inherited a substantial sum of money from her parents, there was nothing anyone could say or do about her purchase. She smiled to herself at her first 'real' show of independence.

It was her daily practice to check the hotel reservations to see if any required special attention. Their clientele mostly stayed the same, landowners in town on business, and families celebrating birthdays and wedding anniversaries. On this day, she noted an unfamiliar name. Two names, actually. She was studying the reservation book when the hotel's main door opened, and a man entered.

"Hello there," he said. "You work here?"

Elizabeth frowned at his casual words. "I expect so, since I'm the manageress."

The man appeared to be in his thirties, and wore tweeds with high-cut boots, and a jaunty cap that he removed as he approached the desk. His hair was as black as coal and cut unusually short. While he spoke, he tapped a cane against the woodwork. "Sorry about that, Ma'am, I mistook you for the help."

"What can I do for you?" asked Elizabeth.

"Nothing, but to make sure my reservations are good. William Kendrick is my name."

"Yes, Mr. Kendrick, all is well. Reservations for two people."

"Righto. Johnnie Dunn is the other name in your book. My team is scattered about, but I liked the look of this place. Classy, I'd rightly call it. Who is this Dane person? When we were driving in, I saw the name all over."

"The hotel is owned by the Dane family, I'm Elizabeth Dane. And we own several businesses in town."

He stepped back from the desk. "Won't keep you from your work, Mrs. Dane."

"Miss," said Elizabeth. "Team? What exactly is that?"

"Rugby. Expect in the hotel business you don't know much about rugby."

"You're right about that. Oh, by the way, where is your place of residence? I don't see it mentioned here." She pointed to the book.

"The girl that took my booking didn't ask for it. I'm from Hay in Breconshire, Wales. You probably never heard of the place."

"But I have," said Elizabeth as she noted the new information. "I believe it's on the English border, and if I can recall, a very dark place like lots of towns in Wales." She shut the reservation book with a snap. "Your rooms will be ready at noon tomorrow, Sir."

"Good enough," he said and turned toward the door, where he paused to check an ornate watch attached to his belt. He walked back a few steps, "I don't suppose you'd consider having a spot of tea with me, Miss Dane? I missed my lunch and am quite famished. I like a bit of company when I eat."

Elizabeth glanced at a dainty watch pinned to her blouse. "I'm not sure that I should," she said, hesitating, "since you are a guest." She paused when she saw his sobered expression. "Perhaps I could make an exception since it is tea-time. The Golden Arms is only a few steps away."

It was as if she'd offered him a gold piece.

"I'll get my coat from the back," she said. "I'll only be a minute."

In the hotel dining room, they sat by the window at a table provided for afternoon teas. William ordered a large plate of roast lamb and mashed potatoes covered with gravy. The girl who took his order had appeared startled at the request for a hot dinner rather than small sandwiches and cakes. "I'll have to check the kitchen to see if anything is left from noon," she said, quickly disappearing.

When she returned, she took Elizabeth's order for tea and a sweet bun. "They're making up a hot plate for you, Sir," she said turning to William.

When their food arrived, Elizabeth said, "Mr. Kendrick. Tell me a little about your Welsh Rugby team? What position do you play?"

He chuckled. "Since we're eating in a companionable way, call me William, or Will as my mates do. My position on the team? I'm what's called a 'playing captain', have been for going on five years."

"That sounds important," Elizabeth said, with nothing better to say.

He smiled in a cocky way.

"And you play all over?"

He forked up the last of his meal. "Mostly in Wales. We're here because we beat the English team."

Elizabeth set down her teacup. "I expect that made your team happy."

"That it did. We're here for a rematch. They want us to beat them all over again."

"Being English, I'm not sure I'd want that," said Elizabeth, and she pushed back her chair, preparing to leave. "I must be going," Mr., ah, William. "I'll be at the desk when you check in tomorrow. Enjoy your evening."

"Excuse me for not seeing you out," he said. "I want to keep an eye out for my mate. He should be walking by shortly. We'll be having a whiskey together, maybe two."

"That sounds enjoyable." She shook his hand.

She passed the hotel and walked toward home. It had been a long time since she'd found any man as interesting as this Welshman. George would likely call him uncouth, professional sports being in the same category as the theatre, or worse. But George was not here.

Elizabeth could not get William Kendrick out of her mind. She planned to be at the hotel when he checked in the next day. Unfortunately, a parcel to be delivered to the townhouse was delayed, and she did not get to the hotel until after 1:00 p.m. William and his teammate had checked in and then left. There was no sign of either of them the following day or the next. The woman at the front desk said William had paid his bill shortly after noon, and the last she saw of him, he was high tailing up the street.

Elizabeth relieved the woman at the desk, and through the afternoon settled down to going over hotel accounts. She had just made a cup of tea prior to going home when the hotel main door open and William waltzed in. Obviously, he'd been celebrating and was quite tipsy.

"Hello there, Miss Elizabeth Dane." He grabbed hold of a chair to steady himself. "The English lads weren't up to fighting off the black Welsh miners."

"So, you're telling me you won?"

"That we did, fair and square."

"Why are you here? I gather you checked out earlier."

He regained his balance. "So, you noticed. Couldn't leave town without saying farewell to the fair and lovely Miss Dane." He chuckled. "Like most Welshmen, I'm a poet."

"I notice."

He had changed out of earlier tweeds, into dove gray trousers and a jacket of Sherwood green and was minus his cap and cane. "I could do with a cup of what you have, if you could spare the time to make it."

"I was just leaving to go home." This man seemed used to getting his own way. "I suppose before I leave, I could make you tea, from the look of you, you certainly need it. Find a seat by the door, I'll bring it to you."

He was humming a tune when she handed over a mug of tea. "I've used a mug because I don't want one of my cups broken and scattered all over the floor."

He drank the tea in three gulps.

"Would you care for more?"

"No, one mug of the brew is enough for me at any time. Ugly stuff."

"You'd better leave for home before too late, and not drink anymore whiskey. You'll be run off the road."

"I'm catching an overnight coach," he said. "Have to have a meal first. I came hoping you'd join me?"

"Really? You can hardly stand up."

"Course, I can…well, maybe after another mug of tea. Does that mean you'll have a spot of supper with me—like I said before, I don't like eating alone."

"If you promise not to drink while you're in my company, I will dine with you," she said stiffly. Fortunately,

George was still away and there was no chance he'd see her with the Welshman.

William took her arm as they left the hotel and walked the short distance to the Golden Arms. Inside, she chose seats well back from the main door. When the young girl who had served them earlier came to their table, she said in a cheeky way, "So you're back, m'lord. Are you looking for another hot meal?"

He quickly checked the menu. "No, I think a cold roast beef sandwich will do the trick. And a glass of milk, as well."

The young girl gushed, "Can't change your mind, Sir?" She poured him a glass of water. "Is there anything else?"

"Not today, little lady," he said, patting her hand.

"William!" Elizabeth had watched this playful exchange.

"Having a bit of fun," said William. "Don't get your britches in a knot."

"I'd rather you had your fun on your own time," said Elizabeth with a humph. She ordered tea and lemon tarts from the girl who pouted in a very unbecoming way.

When their food arrived, Elizabeth said, "I'd like to hear more about your family? When I was a child, my father had business that took him to the border towns, and I went with him. When you're not playing rugby, what do you do? Have you a vocation?"

"My dad's a master linen weaver, turned tailor, with a shop in town. I never learned the weaving, but, Thomas, my dad, taught me the ins and outs of the shop. I work there when I'm not playing rugby. Besides that, I'm a member of the Militia."

"And your mother? Is she alive?"

William finished his sandwich, and the last of the milk, and pushed the dishes aside.

"Dad's been married twice. His first wife, Ann, died early after they had several children together. The only one I know well is my half-sister, Annie who married a local fellow. They live in Hay."

"Then after a year or so, Dad married Lucy, that's my mother. There's eight of us all told. Her family have lived in the area for generations."

"My goodness, there are as many in your family as there are in mine." Elizabeth folded her serviette and placed it beside her plate. "If you're finished, I should get back to the hotel. Is your friend Johnnie catching the same coach tonight?"

"No, I'm on my own. Johnnie is going up north to visit relatives. I expect I'll sleep most of the way home."

As William walked Elizabeth back to the hotel, he took her hand. "I don't have any games scheduled up this way, but Evesham is not all that far. If I'm in the area, shall I drop by the hotel to say hello?"

"Why don't you do that—if you're in town—I'm always ready for a cup of tea."

He laughed heartedly. "You and your tea! Goodbye, then, until another time."

She watched him turn off Main Street toward Carriage House, where likely while waiting to leave, he'd have a whiskey and soda.

George arrived home a few days later, and in his usual manner, when he'd been away, he stopped by the townhouse to see Elizabeth. He refused a cup of tea, asked for a sherry instead. Then he got to the matter that was bothering him.

"Sophie was in town picking up something from the dressmaker earlier in the week. She intended stopping at the hotel to say hello, then she noticed you a half block away, a man holding your arm. Someone we know in town visiting?"

"Not exactly, George." Elizabeth concocted a small white lie. "A guest, new to town, was looking for a tearoom. I decided to show him my favorite place and have a cup at the same time. He was holding my arm, afraid I'd stumble. You know how there's a few bad patches in the sidewalk. Tell Sophie she should have caught up with us, joined us for tea."

"Yes, I'll do that." He looked at her oddly, then let it go and related a few bits of gossip from his travels.

Busy body were the first words that came to Elizabeth's mind after George left.

She could not get the Welshman out of her mind as much as she tried. His home was many hours away, and it was unlikely she would see him again. She began to read the sport's news in the Evesham Weekly. The game of rugby was rarely mentioned.

Then one day in late June, William unexpectedly arrived at the hotel along with two other men, all dressed alike in tight-bottomed trousers, polished boots, and short matching jackets. William came up to the counter, while the other two stood at the door. "We're passing through, so I only have a minute, on the way to a rendezvous up north with the Militia. How are you?"

"I am well, thank you."

"Good. Look, I'm busy for the rest of the week, then I'm done. I'd like to stop by and see you before heading home?"

Her heart leaped. "Yes, will you stay long enough to have a meal? If you think it's appropriate, I could ask my housekeeper to prepare a lunch, or dinner. How will I know which day you're arriving?"

"I'll get a message off to you," he said as he started for the door.

Five days later a messenger boy dropped off an envelope to say that William would be in town the following day and would meet her at the hotel. The dinner at the townhouse became one of many over the next year.

Shortly after Elizabeth's thirty-first birthday, William asked Elizabeth for permission to speak to her family about formally courting her. She spoke to George, who knew something was going on, and they set a date for dinner at the Dane house. Elizabeth had butterflies in her stomach until the day arrived.

William was equally worried. He felt he had several strikes against him. Compared to the Dane family with establishments as far away as London, he had nothing. His father had pointed this out. "There's lots of local girls you could have courted," he said. "They'd be jumping up and down for your attention, but, no, you had to look for a girl out of your class. I hope you know what you're doing."

Then there was the business of being a professional rugby player. William was smart enough to know this rated low in the class system.

And if all of this wasn't enough, he was a Welshman. Despite many of his countrymen moving to England, lots of English had no time of day for the Welsh.

William arrived in Evesham the morning of the dinner, staying at a small hotel on the edge of town. He'd packed a black tailored suit complete with vest, white shirt, and ruby red tie. Not having proper shoes, as soon as he arrived, he'd bought oxfords.

When he knew the date for the dinner with the Danes', he'd said to his dad's tailor in the shop, "Make me a suit on a rush job, Tommy, I need to look like a gentleman." Now, smiling at his reflection in the hotel mirror, he decided he was a gentleman fit for a funeral. Fortunately, the evening was warm, and he needed nothing more than his suit jacket.

Elizabeth had chosen a simple gown and matching jacket for the dinner. She was at the window of the townhouse watching for William, and her heart lurched at the sight of him striding toward the door. Used to him being casually dressed, she barely recognized the smartly attired man approaching. And she was a bit relieved at his appearance.

George Dane and his wife, Sophie, lived on the outskirts of town in a two-story gabled home built a century ago, but recently modernized. It was surrounded by a high fence that kept intruders out, but Elizabeth knew the secret to opening the gate, and she quickly unlocked it.

William was overwhelmed, although he tried to hide the fact. He followed Elizabeth up the graveled path, and steps to the front door. She rang the bell. Expecting a maid, William was surprised when a middle-aged woman opened the door, and Elizabeth hugged her and turning to William said, "I'd like you to meet my sister-in-law, Sophie."

They were seated in the parlor when George appeared, casually dressed. Immediately, William felt overdressed. It was then and there, he decided he would not allow George Dane to intimidate him. George offered a variety of before dinner drinks, and William chose a whiskey and soda. Over small talk, George said, "The name Kendrick? I don't believe we have anyone by that name in town." He looked questionably at William.

"Not likely you would," said William, "it being a fine old Welsh name dating back centuries. According to my da, it means a chief." He cast a quick glance at Elizabeth.

"Curious," said George. "I thought it was only Scotland that had chiefs." He turned to the dining room door where the maid waited to announce dinner.

William stared at his dinner plate surrounded by an array of cutlery. With Elizabeth seated beside him, he was able to watch which fork or spoon she chose—or wine glass, because there were two above the placemat. Finally, the meal—as he'd expected, roast beef, and all the trimmings, and a pudding—ended. They were about to go back to the parlor when George said, "I expect William and I need to talk. We'll join you ladies shortly."

About a half hour later, after Elizabeth joined Sophie with a dry sherry, the men returned to the parlor. George poured two drinks from the sideboard and handed one to William. "Cheers," he said. He didn't sit down again, and neither did William.

With a tight little smile George said, "Well, I expect you two want to get going before it's too late. You'll think about everything we talked about, William?"

At the door George kissed Elizabeth on the cheek and shook hands with William. Sophie stayed in the parlor.

"Thank God that's over," said William under his breath as they walked down the path to the gate.

Back at the townhouse, William shed his suit jacket, and kicked off the oxfords that were hurting his feet and left them at the front door. "I don't want many of those evenings," he said, pulling Elizabeth close. "Before he gives us a blessing that brother of yours wants me to make a few changes in my life. Mainly, saying goodbye to my game. My pals aren't going to be pleased to hear that."

"I knew George would want that," said Elizabeth. "What else?"

"Find myself what he considers a proper job after the courting is done. Even offered to help set me up in something. Brother or not, Elizabeth, I don't much like the man."

William followed Elizabeth into the small sitting room off the entrance, used more often than the parlor. She poured two glasses of sherry. "Sorry, it's all I have. Sit down, William, forget about George."

"How can I forget a man who treated me like he was hiring a gardener? Look at the way he was dressed, and me in a bloody suit, which, I might add, cost a bloody mint." He ignored the fact he'd received a discount from his dad's shop.

He finished the sherry in one gulp, poured another from the decanter on the table, and sat with his stockinged feet stretched out before him.

"George means well, William. I know he can be rather stuffy at times, it's his way," said Elizabeth, taking a chair beside him.

"Maybe, but he's got the manners of a lout. And he insulted me offering to set me up."

"Yes, tonight wasn't the time for that. Besides, I have plenty of funds to invest. We won't need George's money."

"How long is this courtship supposed to last?" William changed the subject.

"Usually, a couple looks at about a year, but since we've been seeing each other more than six months, I expect another six would suffice."

"Good. I'll wind up my affairs back home—Dad will need to find someone to replace me in the shop. Since I'll be moving to England, the rugby will take care of itself. And I'll investigate places for sale—a men's wear, would be ideal."

"I'd best be going. I'm catching the first coach out in the morning to get me home for a four o'clock game." He kissed her on the cheek, then lightly on the mouth. "I'll be back in three weeks' time, my dear. Don't worry, everything will work out."

Elizabeth avoided George for a week, then she called on Sophie, and on leaving sent her regards to George. Other than saying that William was good looking in a dark sort of way like most of the Welsh, they talked of the families they had in common.

William came for a visit in three weeks, and then on a regular basis for the next three months. On the last occasion he suggested they talk about wedding plans. He said he'd leave the details up to her, only that he'd prefer a small wedding. That suited Elizabeth. "I'm not twenty years old," she said with a smile, "Small is the right way to go."

The other request William had was to include his home in Hay on their honeymoon. "I want you to meet my dad and mother."

They were married on a September day in 1893 at the church she occasionally attended. Fifty people attended the wedding and reception, including the brothers and wives who lived in the area, and a few family friends. Several of William's teammates came to the wedding, but no family. George offered to host the reception, but Elizabeth said she preferred to have it at the Grande Hotel. Following the event, the couple left for Hay. They were barely seated in the coach when William shed his suit jacket, and tie, and untied the oxfords he'd been compelled to wear. He produced his high-topped boots from a bag at his feet, and turning to Elizabeth said, "That's better, I'm more like myself."

As agreed, the couple took the overnight coach to the Welsh border, where they transferred to a smaller one to drive into Hay for a one-night stay at the Lion Hotel situated in the heart of the town. After lunch, they strolled down the town's main street, and William pointed out various places of interest. The town was known for its bookstores, many selling old volumes as well as newer ones. William lingered outside one of the shops while Elizabeth browsed through the selections, choosing two.

"My dad will be finished his meal, back at the shop," William said, and he took her arm. "Ma helps out a woman in town to make a bit of extra money. We'll catch her later."

The Thomas Kendrick shop with a neat metal sign above the door, was fitted in between two larger stores. Inside, a man was cutting fabric at a long table. William called out, "Tommy, take a break, and meet my new wife, Elizabeth. Is my dad about?"

Tommy put his scissors aside, and he extended his hand to Elizabeth. "You'll have your hands full with this boyo," he said, with a grin. "Don't let him get away with anything." He turned to a door at the back of the shop. "I'll tell your dad you've arrived, Willy."

The door to the back of the shop opened and a man rushed out. "You're here all in one piece, my boy. You didn't get eaten up by the English!"

"Ah, come off it, Dad. Don't forget I've got an English bride." Elizabeth looked at the two of them standing side by side, mirror images of each other despite Thomas' gray hair.

"Don't mind me," Thomas said, and he took her hand. "William, your mother's been checking the calendar each day, better go over to the house right away. I'll finish up here and catch you later."

"Your father is a cheerful man," Elizabeth said as they left the shop.

"He's a happy sort all right." William directed her past the hotel, and up the hill to the family home. "Don't expect much," he said, as they turned into a narrow street with row houses.

The Kendrick cottage was set back from the street, and like all the others had a brick exterior except for one wall that sided the neighbors. William saw her looking at this. "Would have to be as skinny as a church mouse to crawl in there. We had to leave the old stone facing." He stepped up to the cottage door and opened it. "Ma? You about?"

A woman, as round as a ruffled banty hen, came to greet William, enfolding him in her arms. She turned to Elizabeth, and said, shyly, "I'm Lucy Kendrick. Welcome." She was about sixty years old, showing signs of the pretty girl she had once been before childbirth took its toll.

"Thank you," said Elizabeth. "I'm pleased to be here."

Inside a room that appeared to be a kitchen, William lifted a cloak from a chair and hung it on a peg by the door. "I see you just got home, Ma. We stopped at the shop and had a few words with Da. He'll be home shortly." He indicated to Elizabeth to sit in the chair now clear of the cloak. "Have you any tea, Ma? Elizabeth loves a spot of tea."

After welcoming Elizabeth, Lucy stared, transfixed. She jumped at William's request. "I do, very good leaves, too." She hurried to a cupboard above the kitchen sink, returning with a dainty teacup and saucer, and a heavy glass of whiskey for William. She produced a plate of biscuits.

"Dad told me you've been marking the calendar for our wedding day?"

She nodded, cocking her head as if waiting for him to continue.

While Elizabeth sipped her tea and ate a biscuit, William told his mother about the wedding and reception and the hotel where he stayed. She nodded from time to time, taking it all in.

While they visited, Elizabeth looked around the room. She saw a small parlor off where they were sitting and a short hall with several doors. The cottage was larger than it first appeared. While mother and son chatted, Elizabeth returned her cup and saucer to the kitchen counter, and on the way back to the chair noticed a tablecloth, the embroidery half finished, draped over a chair.

Lucy had left off talking with William to stand behind Elizabeth. "It's for you," she said, "a wedding present for you and William, but I haven't finished it."

"It's beautiful—perfect, stitches so small. A gift like this is worth waiting for, and William can bring it home after he visits you."

Lucy's face lighted up at the praise.

Shortly after, Thomas arrived home, and he moved the four of them into the parlor, where he poured an amber liquid into small glasses. "Is this your own brew, Da?" asked William. "If it is, I should warn Elizabeth that it's pretty potent."

In answer, Thomas smiled, and since the afternoon was approaching the dinner hour, he suggested they finish their drinks and go to the pub.

"Good idea," said William. "That will be handy for us staying at the Lion." Back at the hotel, William suggested they stay another day in Hay to look around at the sights.

This was their first night together, and Elizabeth was nervous. Carrying her nightgown and robe she went into the bathroom in the hall to change, returning to find William in undershirt and trousers sitting on the edge of the bed. He'd turned down the lamp, and a pale glow filled the small room.

For all his bravado, and funning with tearoom girls, she saw he was as nervous as she was. They eyed each other like a couple of skittish colts. Then he said, "Come here, me girl. Let's find out what it's all about."

In the morning, when she awoke, tangled in her nightgown, William's side of the bed was empty. Within minutes he appeared with cups and saucers, cream and sugar and a pot of steaming tea. A few biscuits were tucked in beside it all. "For my English bride," he said, with a wide smile, "to start her morning off."

They had a pleasant day in Hay-on-Wye, picnicking on the grass near the river, searching for the castle everyone said they must see. The hotel had packed them a lunch in a wicker basket, making them promise they would not forget to return it.

Elizabeth asked William about his family. Young John and Henry were working in the coal mines, living with their wives close to the work. Lizzie was married and had several children. She lived two hours away. Fanny, born three years before William and never married, lived in town. Also in town was Annie, who'd married the local man. Lucy and Annie had become good friends, only ten years difference in age.

"I like your mother," said Elizabeth. "At first she seemed shy with me."

He pulled her close. "That's because you seem a grand lady to ma. With your fancy clothes and stylish hair and talking to Da about the books you bought in town. Dad had to have some education to take his apprenticeship, but Ma didn't go past the first grades. She can't read or write."

"Oh my, I wouldn't have guessed. She's made her own way, though, with the lovely needle work, and raising a family."

"That she has."

They looked around town in a different direction before returning to the family cottage, where after a short wait, Thomas arrived home. Lucy didn't arrive until later.

William accepted another drink of Thomas' amber liquor, and Elizabeth declined, opting for a cup of Lucy's special tea. The woman had warmed to Elizabeth and offered to show off her needlework, disclosing that she sold some in town along with woven bookmarks for those who had a need for them.

When they left with promises to return soon, Elizabeth carried an exquisitely embroidered handkerchief and a three-color woven runner made by Thomas, who still dabbled in the craft.

They had a quiet dinner in the hotel dining room. William told Elizabeth about the history of Wales, its division from England that went back to Anglo-Saxon times, and about the unrest in the country as they fought for identity.

He changed the subject and spoke about rugby. "It's our national sport, Elizabeth, very important, and hard for me to give up. I guess with me living in England, one hasn't a choice."

"You'll be able to get together with your pals from time to time," she reassured.

He did not answer her.

The next morning instead of going north for another look around the Welsh countryside, they decided to take the coach home. When they arrived, they went directly to the townhouse, surprising the housekeeper, who put together a quick meal. While Elizabeth got organized, William went for a walk to get some air. When he returned, she saw he'd visited a pub. She said nothing about this. Instead, they enjoyed a quiet meal and afterwards Elizabeth went through the mail and messages that came while she was away. While on the honeymoon, Elizabeth had arranged for someone to work in her place at the hotel. "What will you do while I'm out?" she asked William, the next morning.

"I picked up a few of the dailies while out. I plan to check out the ads for properties and what not. Don't worry about me."

"Then I'll see you back here. I should let George know we're home."

"I'm sure his spies will already have told him."

"Hmm. I hope there won't always be trouble between the two of you."

"Not on my part. I'll simply avoid him," said William.

They settled into a routine, Elizabeth going to the hotel mid-morning, returning early in the afternoon. William seemed to put in his time, although she wasn't sure what he did or where he went? Then one day he laid a newspaper on the table and pointed to a boxed ad. "This is worth a look. What do you think?"

The advertisement was for a men's wear shop, situated about halfway up High Street, a short distance from the hotel. "Says, it has steady customers, and a tailor on the premises. Family business for twenty-five years."

"I'll go with you, Will. What are they asking?"

"Doesn't say, not a good sign."

"We don't know until we ask," she said, getting her coat from the rack. As they walked up the street she said, "We've never discussed finances, Will. Do you have money set aside to invest in a business?"

He hesitated. "Not as much as I hoped. When I was home Dad touched me up for a bit of a loan. He had to help out one of the boys, it left him short for taxes."

"Oh. Well, we need not worry until we talk to the owner of this business advertised. I'd want to check out the books before we invest in anything."

"That's your department," Will said.

The shop was mid-sized in a good location, with large windows that faced the street, everything tidy. "Might as well go in," said Elizabeth, "no point standing out here."

No sooner were they inside when they were approached by a middle-aged man, nattily dressed, a good sign. Elizabeth stepped back to let William take the initiative to discuss a sale. But when she saw he was giving the impression they were merely lookers, and not serious buyers, she stepped forward, and introduced herself, giving her maiden name along with her married one. The man, Harry Landers, brightened after hearing the Dane name. "George Dane and I belong to the same lodge," he said. "I see him at least once a month."

Elizabeth explained that she was newly married, and they required a family business. Harry Landers invited them into his office, told them his asking price for the business, discussed sales, and where he purchased his fabrics.

When Elizabeth saw she was running late to get to the hotel, she ended the discussion by saying, "Sounds like your business is exactly what we want. My husband and I will talk this over this evening and get back to you quickly. She did not have to ask to see the company books; Landers offered them to her to review.”

When they arrived at the hotel, Elizabeth said, “Will, come in for a minute, we need to talk. You didn’t have much to say in the shop.”

“When I heard what he was asking, I had nothing to say.”

“One never pays the asking price, Will. You might as well tell me how much you have saved, so I can do some figuring?”

After a pause, looking uncomfortable, he said. “I can find fifty pounds, give or take.”

Looking thoughtful, she said. “I was hoping for more. We need at least twice that. This means I’ll have to make up the rest. I know you don’t want to ask George.”

“Not on your life!”

“All right, let’s leave the discussion for now, talk again tonight. Were you satisfied with the look of the place?”

“I’ve nothing against it.”

“What do you plan to do for the rest of the day?”

“Two of my mates are in town. We’re getting together for a chin wag.”

“Then, I won’t worry about you. I’ll be home in good time.” Elizabeth left the hotel early due to an upset stomach which persisted through the evening. She still felt unwell and delayed talking to William about buying the shop until after breakfast, the next morning.

“Something’s upset my stomach,” she told him, as she nibbled a bit of dry toast. “I’m going to take the day off.”

He looked up from reading the morning news. "I've done my own calculating. I figure I can come up with more like seventy pounds."

She pushed away her plate, suddenly nauseated, and rushed from the breakfast room. "Sorry, about that," she said when she returned. "Seventy pounds would be a great help. I'll add up the figures later, right now I must lie down."

By noon, feeling restored, she made herself a light lunch, and while she ate, she started to think. They had been married three months, had not used any protection. With an upset stomach and early morning nausea, she likely was pregnant. She decided to keep the news to herself, at her age one never knew the outcome.

When William returned to the house late afternoon, she was sitting at the dining room table, surrounded by paper. "Come and join me, Will, and I'll show you what I've been doing. Would you bring me a small sherry, please?"

He set the glass before her and slid into the chair across, a shot glass before him. For an hour, they talked back and forth about the purchase, finally deciding with Elizabeth topping up Williams' contribution, they could purchase the business on High Street.

"Wonderful!" She tipped her glass to his. "The shop will keep you busy. We'll go first thing in the morning to make our offer."

Without hesitating, Harry Landers accepted their offer of one half down, and the remainder to be paid over twenty-four months. They agreed on one month to the day to assume ownership.

"Have you thought of a name for the shop?" asked Elizabeth as, arm in arm, they walked home.

"I've hardly digested buying it," said William. "Have you any ideas?"

"William Kendrick's Men's Wear," she said without hesitation.

"Bit of a handle," Will said. "Expect the town will know it as Kendrick's."

"Agreed."

This was January 1894. A month later, the same day that Harry Landers handed William the keys to the shop, Elizabeth miscarried without ever telling him she was expecting. She had felt poorly for a day, and stayed quietly at home, and felt no remorse at the loss. She wanted to help William establish the clothing business in his own right, not have to contend with a newborn. She was content to know there would be another time.

Kendrick's Men's Wear flourished, and William seemed happy. He'd discarded his casual attire, and now donned a suit each day to go to the shop, although he refused to wear oxfords and had found more comfortable footwear.

Elizabeth cut back the hotel hours and hired another girl. She had found a gardener to redo the back area of the townhouse, planting her favorite flowers including an array of lilies. Occasionally, she wondered why she hadn't got pregnant again. She and Will certainly enjoyed plenty of intimate time.

Then in July of that year, the familiar nausea, tiredness arrived. She waited two months to tell Will the news. He was as happy as she was. Other than a small scare with some spotting, the pregnancy was uneventful. At six months, she cut back her hours at the hotel, and continued to reduce them until a few weeks before the baby was expected, when one morning she awoke with discomfort in her back. She had not been sleeping well and attributed the pain to tossing and turning all night. When the ache persisted, she asked Will, on his way to the shop, to alert the doctor.

Old Dr. Bradley had been the attending physician for all the Dane babies. He was well in his seventies and did not mind that Elizabeth planned to have Sally Sparrow, a midwife, deliver her baby, with him available if needed. He was knocking at the townhouse door within an hour. An examination revealed the baby was on its way. "I'll get a message off to Sally," he said.

Lilianna Kendrick arrived ten hours later. The doctor was not needed.

Every day, Elizabeth saw a difference in Lily, as if like her namesake, she unfolded. Her eyes began to focus on her surroundings, especially on Elizabeth, who no longer worried that the infant would survive.

Three weeks after she was born, Elizabeth asked Will when he was going to register Lily's birth. This required going to the courthouse in a town an hour away. He looked up from his breakfast of bacon and eggs, and said, "I'll do it tomorrow, Elizabeth. A salesman from a London house is arriving today to show me a new line of fabrics."

"Perhaps you should write a reminder to yourself."

The next day as he prepared to leave the house, he said, "It would be helpful if you jotted down the particulars on Lily, to jog my memory. I'm planning to take care of the registration after I check in at the shop."

Prepared for this, Elizabeth handed him a paper with Lily's full name, birth weight and date of birth. Will tucked the paper into his back pocket.

It was close to noon before he left the shop to make the hour drive to the courthouse, which was closed for the dinner hour. Rather than hang around outside, he found a pub nearby and settled down. After a hearty meal and two whiskies, he returned to the courthouse, now open, although the clerk said they closed in less than an hour.

Will checked for the paper Elizabeth gave him, searching every pocket. There was no sign of it, likely dropped when he paid for his dinner. Sheepishly, he said to the clerk who waited, "Can't seem to find the particulars, will have to rely on my memory."

"Name? We call her Lily; full name is Lilianna." He wracked his brain for the second name, gave up on it. "Weight? Just a bit of a thing, let's say three pounds." Date born? "That's a good one," he mused. "I had to go to the garden to tend to Lion, my hound—about three weeks ago, must have been March 13. Jot that down, my good man. What does a day or two matter?" He was at the door when the other name came to him. "Sarah!" He called back to the clerk. "The babe's name is Sarah Lilianna."

Will returned to the pub where he'd enjoyed his noon dinner. "A whiskey and make it quick. I have to catch the last coach," he said.

The years moved along—In **1896**, Will hired two more employees for the shop, and established a new clothing line. The nursemaid was no longer needed. Elizabeth took over Lily's entire care. She also informed her family to make new arrangements for the hotel since she was unable to manage it now that she was a mother.

In **1897**, Elizabeth gave birth to a son that they named Frederick William. Lily doted on her baby brother helping Elizabeth by carrying in nappies, and baby formula.

In **1898,** Will started to take Lily to the walled gardens, where she played with the spotted hound, Lion, who was becoming grizzled with age. They travelled from the townhouse by pony and cart, and Lily never stopped chattering.

In **1899,** the Dane family began to plan for next year's gala celebration when the calendar welcomed in a new century. That same year, Elizabeth, registered Lily in an exclusive girl's academy. Having seen the wrong date on Lily's birth certificate, Elizabeth was annoyed. When she saw the mistake, she had words with Will. "How could you forget the date your daughter was born?"

Will had started calling her Bessie like the rest of the family. "Now don't get yourself twisted in a knot, Bessie." he said. "It's a small thing." The mistake still bothered her, but not wanting to quarrel with Will, she let it go.

The hotel lived up to its name with a grand event when January 1st, 1900, arrived. The brothers from London closed shop for two days and returned to Evesham to celebrate. Elizabeth worried how Will would react with so many of her family, but he surprised her with his best behavior. He wore a custom-made suit, the fabric newly arrived from Italy, and pointed toed shoes like men were wearing in Europe. He was easily the best dressed man in the room, and, oh, so handsome.

Following the New Year's celebration, Lily started school at the academy. She looked very serious in her navy uniform and white blouse with a red tie at her neck as she waited for her mother to accompany her on the first day. From then on, her father would take her to school since brother, Freddy, could not be left alone.

Although Lily was healthy, never having a sick day, she was a small boned, petite child with auburn ringlets that Elizabeth wrapped in rags for special occasions, such as the first day of school. Despite her small stature, she had a strong mind of her own. William doted on her. He was pleased he had a son, but, in his heart, there was no one like his little precious Lily.

Starting Lily in school midterm, well before her fifth birthday, gave her an edge on beginning in September. She was advanced for her age, had learned the alphabet, and her numbers up to 100. She was used to hearing her father say, "You're a clever girl."

She quickly made friends with several girls in her class, and when her mother asked who she would like to invite to her birthday party in March, she listed five girls right off. Elizabeth decided to use the middle date between actual birth date and that on the mistaken birth certificate, which happened to be a Saturday, for the party. She printed the invitations with Lily at her elbow, making sure she got it right.

Will arranged pony rides for the six children, and Elizabeth found a variety of games to play at the house. Lily accompanied her mother to the bakery to choose the cake, chocolate with an abundance of swirled whipped cream and miniature lady fingers.

The day went off perfectly, just as perfect as Lily in a new starched dress as yellow as the daffodils in the garden. Elizabeth looked on satisfied; William beamed.

The school term was scheduled to end in May, concluding with an assembly to hand out certificates. William took time off from the shop and met Elizabeth at the school. Lily received a scrolled diploma for work ethics—she had to ask her father what ethics meant—and another diploma for congeniality. "They shouldn't use so many big words," she said on the walk home. Elizabeth was inclined to agree.

"What am I going to do now there's no school?" she asked the next morning. Elizabeth suggested they make Welsh cakes, and instead of cooking them on the stove, they'd light the fireplace to bake them. Lily clapped her hands, "I can help, Momma."

Elizabeth mixed the batter, with Lily sprinkling in the currants. Kindling in the fireplace had started to take. Freddy going on four, was getting in the way, and sent to his room to play. "I'll just see to Freddy for a minute, then we'll do the cooking. Your father will be pleased, he loves Welsh cakes." She left the room.

Too long, Lily thought, I'll make a special cake for Dada, and she carried the pan to the fireplace.

She leaned over the fire to poke at the wood. A spark flew up and landed on the collar of her high-necked velvet dress. She brushed at the spark, but it had caught the lace and was burning her neck. She dropped the pan that held the single cake and leaned over to retrieve it. Another spark landed in her hair.

"Momma," she screamed, as she frantically brushed at the flames that seemed to be crawling up her body.

"No, oh no!" Elizabeth grabbed a braided mat and rolled Lily in it to douse the flames. Hearing the noise, Freddy ran into the room. "Run, run, next door for help." She unwrapped the mat and stared at Lily. Ugly red patches were already forming on her neck and face.

The neighbor was familiar with Elizabeth's family doctor. She sent a message immediately to old Doctor Bradley whose own health was poor, forcing him to semi retire, and take only a few patients, which included the Dane family. He arrived, out of breath, took one look at Lily and shook his head. "Not good," he said. "I see you have removed her dress."

Elizabeth stood back out of the doctor's way. The neighbor had arrived and taken charge of Freddy. She whispered to Elizabeth, "I'll take the lad to my house until his father gets home."

"He went over to the garden as he usually does on a Sunday."

The doctor had carried Lily onto the couch and finished his examination. "The child is in shock, Elizabeth, she should go to the hospital, and be treated there."

"No! Hospitals are for the dying. She will stay here in her own home. What can you do for her, Doctor? And tell me what I can do."

"Get a jug of cool water, and bring me cotton batting, petroleum jelly, too, if you have it. I have medication with me, to help her sleep, and ease the pain. I'll return tonight. Have you contacted your husband?"

"I'll send a message to the gardener."

Elizabeth covered Lily with a soft blanket up to her waist. The medication was taking effect, and the child had closed her eyes. Her hair and eyebrows were singed, and the doctor had applied ointment to her neck and lower face, then covered the area with a light bandage. She looked like the victim of a carriage accident. But that didn't change Elizabeth's mind about the hospital. She'd have nothing to do with the place.

She was sitting beside Lily, holding her hand, when Will rushed in the door. "What's happened? The messenger said there'd been an accident at home." His eyes turned to the still form on the couch. "Lily? Oh, my darling girl— Elizabeth? What's happened?"

"She was trying to bake a Welsh Cake for you. The doctor wants to admit her to the hospital. I said, no."

"Why was she at the fire? Where were you?"

"I was only gone a minute. I left her shaping the little cakes. I will never forgive myself." Suddenly, tears gushed from her eyes. "My poor darling."

William stood as if turned to stone. He looked at Elizabeth, then at Lily, wheeled around and left the room. She heard the door to his study close and knew everything had been left up to her.

The accident happened in the morning, and Lily slept most of the afternoon, then Elizabeth, who'd tried to remain calm, heard Lily call out. "Momma?"

"I'm right here Lily."

"Will you let me help you upstairs to my bedroom onto the couch, so you will be more comfortable? I want you by my side tonight." The tears slid down her cheeks as she spoke.

"Don't cry, Momma. You never cry. The fire was nasty. It burned up the Welsh cake I was giving Dada. Bad fire."

"Is the ointment helping the burns?" Elizabeth lifted an edge to the wrapping.

"My face hurts."

"After you've moved to the bedroom, I want you to try and sleep some more. I'm giving you a little bit of the medicine the doctor left. He's coming back this evening. You're a brave girl, Lily."

After Elizabeth settled Lily, and saw her eyes drooping, she went into the kitchen to make a cup of tea. The bowl of batter sat on the counter. She dumped it into the garbage. There had been no sign or sound of William. She doubted she'd see him tonight.

Lily was asleep when the doctor arrived. He appeared weary and his steps were slow. He applied the ointment and rewrapped the bandage on Lily's neck. "She looks a little better tonight, and a good sleep will help," he said.

"Dr. Bradley, I've made fresh tea, would you like a cup before you leave?"

"I wouldn't say no." He followed her downstairs into the kitchen. "Were you able to reach William? I'm sure he was upset."

Elizabeth poured two cups of tea and handed one to the doctor. "He was more than upset. He was in much the same shock as Lily. He's in his study; I don't want to disturb him."

"Just as well." The doctor finished his tea and set the cup aside. "Well, I'll be off, Elizabeth, you need your rest too. Keep on applying the ointment to keep the burn soft, and I'll pop by tomorrow."

She saw him to the door. "You're looking tired tonight, Doctor Bradley. Are you alright?"

He smiled, "As right as an old man can be."

Elizabeth locked the front door and lowered the hall light. She paused at the door to Williams' study, her hand on the doorknob. It was hours since she had seen or heard from him. Quietly, she entered the room. He was stretched out on the settee, fast asleep, his shoes on the floor, an empty glass on the table. She quietly returned to the hall.

Then she made her rounds for the rest of the house, latching the kitchen door, on upstairs to tuck a blanket around Freddy who always kicked the covers off. Satisfied the house was in order, she entered her bedroom. Lily was sleeping peacefully. With the grace of God, she would recuperate.

On and off through the night, Elizabeth tended Lily, applying the ointment to her lips, which had been like rosebuds, but were now starting to pucker. She barely thought of William, so engrossed was she in caring for Lily. When morning came, Lily was sleeping peacefully, allowing Elizabeth to go downstairs for her morning tea. The sun was up, promising a warm June day.

She was cooking the porridge in the hope she could entice Lily to take a spoonful, when the breakfast room door opened, and Will entered. He looked terrible, the start of a beard darkening his face, eyes bloodshot, hair unruly. He took a chair at the table across from her and for a moment said nothing then, "I didn't mean to blame you, Bessie. I wasn't thinking straight." He poured a mug of tea from the pot. "I can't remember being so distressed. How is Lily this morning?"

"The burns on her arm and shoulder appear better, but I'm worried about her lower lip. I'll ask the doctor if there is more, I can do?"

He cut the crust off a new loaf of bread and spread butter and honey. "Like I said, I'm quite beside myself. You remember my mate, Johnnie? He's on his way north for a game. I thought I might ride up with him. Would you be all right if I'm away for a day?"

"I suppose so. I'm going to call the girl who helped when Freddy was born. Will you see Lily before you leave?"

"Of course." Carrying his mug, he left the room, returning a short while later. "She's sleeping. I kissed her on the cheek, poor, wee child."

Will was dressed, shaved and out of the house before she knew it. In a way, she was relieved he was gone.

Word of the accident was soon around town. Sophie was the first to arrive. She clucked, clucked when she saw the burns on Lily's body. Second to arrive was a teacher from the school. She brought a picture book for Lily. The arrival of Maggie, the nursemaid, was a godsend. She had Lily out of her nightie, into a loose smock, sitting in a chair in Elizabeth's bedroom. "No use feeling sorry for yourself," she said, the right approach.

When Elizabeth saw Maggie had everything under control, she said, "I'm going into town to pick up a few things. Tell Lily I'll bring back a treat."

Elizabeth did her shopping, then stopped by the doctor's home. It was odd that she hadn't heard from him. His office door was open, and a man she didn't recognize was behind the desk. "Hello. I'm Mrs. Kendrick. Dr. Bradley is treating my daughter after she was burned in an accident."

He came around from the desk and took her hand. "I've been reading the notes on that. You haven't heard? Doctor Bradley had a stroke last evening, he's been taken to London. Fortunately, I was here when it happened, helping out."

Elizabeth stumbled over her words. "I didn't know. He left me a small jar of ointment, and I'm almost out."

"Why don't I go home with you and examine your daughter? I'm a doctor… well almost. Edinburgh hospitals have new ideas how to treat burn patients, not to say that Dr. Bradley's way isn't right. By the way, I'm James Macleod, newly arrived from Scotland."

Lily was awake, looking at the picture book. A stab of guilt struck Elizabeth, and she wiped at the tears that had started.

"If you are agreeable, Mrs. Kendrick, I'd like to remove the bandages on Lily's neck."

She nodded and held Lily's hand. "One of the new treatments is to allow air to circulate around the burn area," he said, as he took tweezers from his medical bag and began to remove strands of cotton batting from Lily's neck, frowning when a speck of skin came off with the batting. "Petroleum jelly, as Dr. Bradley suggested, is good to use on Lily's lips. And use the same ointment prescribed by Dr. Bradley for the other burns."

He set a full jar on the table.

"Other than that, let time do the healing. Your pretty curls will grow back, as quick as a wink, Lily. I guarantee it."

"Momma wraps my hair in rags to make it curl," Lily said, causing the doctor to smile.

"That little girl of yours has lots of spunk, it will serve her well," the doctor said at the door. "I'll drop by in a day or so, and if there is any problem, call me. I'll be in town until everything is sorted out with Dr. Bradley."

A day later William arrived home in better spirits. He'd brought a large doll for Lily, and several smaller items, and when he saw her downstairs wrapped in a quilt, he was much relieved.

Elizabeth told him about Dr. Bradley's stroke and the new doctor temporarily taking over. "I'm following his suggestions for Lily's treatment. You see the bandages are gone."

"Will she have scars?" He kept his voice low so Lily wouldn't hear.

"I'm hoping they'll disappear in time. So, how did the trip go? I expect it felt good to be around your friends."

"We picked up just like old times. I do miss the game a lot, Bessie."

"I know you do. If there had been any other way…"

"There wasn't." He left the room.

Through the summer Lily recovered her general health. But the ravage of the fire was still apparent, and Elizabeth became despondent. She tried various creams and lotions, several suggested by family and friends, adding gentle massage to lessen the scars on Lily's neck, and make the pucker to her lips disappear. Nothing changed. The only good that came was Lily's hair grew back as abundant as ever.

Lily started talking about school and her friends. Elizabeth wondered how the children would react to Lily's changed face. Will was no help at all. It was Sophie who suggested wrapping Lily's neck in a pretty scarf and she followed up the idea with a gift box of scarves. Still, nothing improved Lily's lip. It was red and puckered and drooped. She would not leave the lip alone, constantly picked at it, making it bleed.

"It will never heal if you don't leave it alone," Elizabeth scolded.

A few days before school started, Lily's teacher came to the house. "I presume Lily will start school as planned?" she said, opening the conversation. "I have an idea I would like to discuss with you. Rather than Lily arriving at 8:30, I would like you to bring her closer to nine. I want time to explain to her classmates that she is recovering from an accident that left scars on her face, and they must not speak of this. I want them to be especially kind to Lily."

"That's good of you to think about this," said Elizabeth and she followed up on the suggestion.

Will nodded when he heard this, but he did say, "Lily must get used to people asking questions about her face. She must be strong. The scars on her neck may never disappear. Her lip may always droop."

Tears sprang to Elizabeth's eyes.

Lily, wearing a new violet colored dress, the same color as her eyes, walked hand in hand with Elizabeth to the Academy.

"I'm only going to see you to the door of your classroom," Elizabeth said. "You're a big girl, and everything will go well."

Lily, who had become more serious since the accident, said, "I see one of my friends, Momma." She dropped Elizabeth's hand.

"I'll be here when school gets out, so off you go."

Classes for first grade lasted until one-thirty, and Elizabeth was there well ahead of the time. Lily emerged from the main door, holding a little girl's hand. She pointed to Elizabeth, said something to her friend, and skipped down the path. Obviously, the teacher's suggestion had worked.

Lily joined a children's choir at school, and piano lessons followed. She took ballet lessons. The scars on her neck were still visible, and her lip still drooped, but none of this affected her outlook on life. She remained a cheerful child.

Children were never a problem. Adults were. They offered suggestions on how to deal with a child with an affliction. Others turned their head as if it was too much for them to bear. And William had trouble coming to terms with Lily's accident. After the first few times when he voiced his opinion, he did not mention it.

One day following Lily's sixth birthday, in the spring of 1901, Elizabeth suggested they take the children to visit their grandparents in Wales. "It's been well over a year since they've seen them." She didn't add that the grandparents had not seen Lily since her accident.

Will tried to change her mind. "They see me often enough. If you want, we could both go, leave the children at home with Maggie."

Elizabeth didn't like to argue with him, but this was one time she forced the issue.

"Seeing me is not the point, Will. I want your parents to get to know our children. Leaving them home will not do that. Besides, when Lily is old enough, she can travel on the train herself."

"Alright. When did you want to do this?"

"I suppose we should wait until school is out for the summer." She knew Will hoped in the months ahead, she would forget about the trip. But she did not. Classes ended, and Lily received several awards, one for achievement. She had little interest in her awards. Elizabeth placed them in an envelope to show the grandparents.

"There's no reason we can't make the trip any time soon, Will. You pick a date. I can't remember when we had a family holiday. You can show Freddy where you learned to play rugby." Freddy was nearly five and would start school in the fall.

Will was forced against the wall. He sent a message to his parents they were coming, booked day passage in the coach, and a family room at the Lion Hotel.

Elizabeth tried to entertain the children on the trip, but by the time they transferred at Hereford to the smaller coach, and had arrived at the hotel in Hay, everyone was exhausted. "I'll drop by the house to let them know we're here," said Will. "We'll take the children over in the morning."

It was late when he returned to the room. The children were in bed, and she was ready to retire. "You go on to bed," Will said. "I'm meeting a couple of the mates downstairs. I won't be long."

Elizabeth did not hear him come to bed, and in the morning when she arose, he was still sleeping. She took the children downstairs for breakfast, and a walk up the street to clear their heads. When they returned to the room with mugs of coffee, instead of the usual tea, Will was sitting half-dressed by the window.

"What time are your parents expecting us?"

"I'll finish this and then get some air. We can go by the house anytime."

The children were playing in the other room. "I expect your parents know about the accident?"

He picked up his clothes from the chair and his shaving kit. "Not in detail. What was the point in worrying them?"

When he returned from the hall bathroom, he was more like himself. "Let's get a move on," he said, taking Freddy's hand.

On the way through town, Elizabeth slipped into the bakery and bought a bag of cream buns. They carried on up the hill to the cottage where the Kendricks lived. The picket fence that surrounded the house had been newly painted in a cheerful green, the steps and door now dark brown. "I see your dad has been busy," she said.

"He's got a bit more time. Said the shop is in a bit of a slump. Had to drop the tailor to half time."

"I'm sorry to hear that. You haven't noticed anything like that at our shop?"

"Sales are down, I didn't bother telling you."

"It's not good to keep it to yourself. I am a part of the business."

With no more to say, he rapped on the door and opened it. Lily and Freddy were hanging back, and Elizabeth pushed them forward. "Don't act like dolts. Give your grandparents a hug."

Lucy wrapped her arms around Lily, then stood back to admire her, a sudden change coming over her face, which quickly she tried to hide. "My, all grown up, I see, and Freddy, you are such a big boy." They moved as a group into the kitchen.

Will was standing next to Thomas. Both men were the same stature, but in the light of the morning, Thomas looked healthier than William. With a jolt, Elizabeth wondered if Will had lost weight without her knowing.

The moment passed. They sat around the kitchen table and Elizabeth produced the cream buns. Conversation turned to the economy of the town, and businesses in general. Lucy invited Elizabeth to a back table where she was working on a piece of embroidery. It must be her imagination, but Lucy also appeared to have lost weight.

"You're keeping well, I hope," said Elizabeth.

"Not too bad. Just getting old," she said. Like Thomas, she was in her sixties.

She pulled Elizabeth aside, and whispered, "Will never told us how bad the accident was. Poor child, to live with those scars for the rest of her life." She lifted the hem of her skirt. Below was a long, jagged scar. "From a tipped tea pot," she said in a matter-of-fact way.

Elizabeth's eyes widened as the sight of a brown mark that extended upward to the thigh. She quickly turned back to the kitchen where Will was gathering the children ready to leave.

"We're going by the park, Dad, to let the children run off their energy. I'll drop by again tonight."

They were quiet as they walked down the hill into town. The park was deserted, and Lily and Freddy ran for the swings, leaving Elizabeth and Will standing alone. He pointed to an adjoining field. "That brings back plenty of memories." He lapsed into silence and continued staring at the field.

Soon tired of the swings, the children ran for a climbing area. Elizabeth watched them play. She was as silent as Will. That evening after supper at the hotel, she said, "I don't think your mother is well, Will. She has lost a lot of weight. Has she mentioned her health to you?"

He paused at door, preparing to go alone to say goodbye to the family. "She hasn't said anything. Probably tired from working extra hours to help out."

"I hope that's all it is." Elizabeth dropped the subject. "Do you plan on staying out late?"

"Not tonight, love. I need my beauty sleep with my beautiful wife—if she'll have me in her bed."

They left for home the next day with Will dozing in the seat beside her and the children working on coloring books.

Five months later, in November, a messenger arrived to say Lucy had passed away from heart failure. Her family were having a private service, and there was no need for Will to make the trip back. Thomas hoped Will would come in the spring when travel was better. When the knock came at the townhouse door with the message Elizabeth and Will had finished their meal. The children had already had their tea and were in the playroom. "I'm not surprised, I knew something was wrong, couldn't put my finger on it," said Elizabeth.

"I should be at the service," said Will.

"Your dad said not to come, besides it's likely over. Better for you to visit your dad in a few months' time. That's when he'll need you."

"I wonder how he'll manage on his own?" said Will. "Maybe our Annie will step in." Annie, Will's half-sister, was now a widow, living on her own in Hay.

Elizabeth cleared the supper dishes. She followed Will into the parlor, and unusual for her, she poured a small sherry from the sideboard. "I'll let you fix your own," she said, pulling a chair close to the fire. "I'll tell the children the news when they're getting ready for bed."

Will poured a brandy and joined her by the fire. "The boys living up at the mine will be terribly upset, being the youngest and all." He lapsed into his own thoughts, and, with the warmth of the fire and the brandy, he fell asleep. Elizabeth finished her sherry and quietly closed the parlor door. She did not expect the children to be overly upset. They hardly knew their grandparents.

With everything that was going on, it was several weeks before Elizabeth had a chance to talk to Will about the decline in their business. When she did, he seemed reluctant to talk about it. She pressed him to be honest with her.

They had returned to the house after looking at a selection of fall bulbs in the potting shed. Will took a small glass from the kitchen cabinet, changed his mind, and returned it to the shelf. He pulled out a chair at the table. "The fact of the matter, Bessie, is that I've had a drop in cash flow. I've already let one man go, and I'm thinking about giving the slip to another."

She threw up her arms. "That's terrible! They're family men. How will they manage?"

"Go on the dole like many others, I expect. Better them than me."

"How much money do you need to clear everything, have a little left over?"

"A couple hundred pounds would do it."

She stood, thinking, "I can't give you that much. The best I can do is one hundred. You know that George manages my personal finances. He'll question anything over a hundred."

"Why is he still involved with your money?"

"It's the way the trust was written. I've never questioned it. My personal needs are simple. When I invested in the business with you, I had to give a reason for withdrawing a large amount."

He shook his head. "It's your money. I still don't understand. All right. If you can get hold of a hundred pounds from dear, old miser George, that will have to do."

A week later Elizabeth handed Will a bank draft for the money. She didn't tell him that it had caused words with her brother, who said, "I won't ask, Bessie, but I hope you have a good reason for needing the money."

On the last Friday of each month Will attended a luncheon with other businessmen. It was held at various dining establishments in town. Following a hearty lunch and several whiskies, he was always in a fine mood, making Elizabeth believe he needed the contact with other men. He always took extra care with how he dressed when he was going out to lunch, never wearing the same suit twice in a row.

After giving Will the money, Elizabeth did not discuss the decline in the business. But several weeks later when he was at the business luncheon, she decided it was a good day to drop in at the shop. She was curious to see if the staff were still the same. Will had appointed Julian Christie as manager, justifying the expense as a necessity to free him for such occasions as the luncheons.

Christie was a small, dapper Frenchman. Elizabeth never had liked him or his manner. "So nice to see you, Mrs. Kendrick," he gushed when she stepped into the shop. "You're out and about early this morning."

"Yes, I try to get my errands finished before noon."

"Is there anything I can help you with? Mr. Kendrick won't be in until later today."

"I know it's his business lunch day. So, Mr. Christie, are you on your own?"

"Unfortunately, yes. This afternoon I have help coming in. As you likely know, business is slow."

"Oh? I thought it had picked up." She walked around looking at displays of racks of ties, handkerchiefs, socks, and various other small items. "I don't recall their names, but are the two men you had no longer employed here?"

Julian Christie picked a stray thread from his jacket, and his manner changed. "As I mentioned, one of the former employees comes in for the afternoon."

"I see." Elizabeth picked up a box of monogrammed handkerchiefs and handed them to him. "I'll take these, Mr. Christie, kindly wrap them since they are a gift." She knew his eyes followed her as she left the shop, pondering what Will had done with the money?

For his own personal use, William took money from the business profits, and he gave Elizabeth cash for the household. Money from the trust fund was deposited twice yearly in Elizabeth's own bank account. This meant that up until now, she did not have to discuss finances with Will.

Not sure how to handle the current matter, for a day or so she did nothing to spoil his good mood. Then, she could wait no longer.

"William, dear, I decided to go by the shop, pick up a small gift for George's birthday. Everything appears neat and tidy, displayed appealingly. As you know, Julian Christie is not my favorite person but that is beside the point. What concerned me was the lack of staff. I thought the money I gave you was going to be used to keep the two men on?"

His lips tightened in annoyance at being questioned. "You do recall I needed two hundred pounds, Elizabeth. I used your money to clear the accounts for two fashion houses. There wasn't any left over."

She pondered the situation for a moment. "If you need to cut back, have you considered letting Mr. Christie go? You could take over managing the shop yourself—you do have the time."

His eyes widened. "Why are you suddenly getting involved in the business? You've always been satisfied to let me handle everything."

Speaking carefully, she said, "I do trust you, Will. It's only a suggestion. I don't mean to upset you."

Elizabeth decided for the time being to drop the matter. With Lily approaching her 10th birthday, she needed to spend more time with the child. Both Freddy and Lily were accomplished in music, taking after their Welsh father, who often joined them in a song. Sometimes, Elizabeth accompanied all three on the piano.

Being part of a large English family insulated Lily from stares and unkind remarks. She was constantly invited to birthday parties, and other social events. Because she moved from grade to grade with the same group of children who accepted the way she looked, she was happy at school. Her whole life revolved around school and being within a few blocks of the family home.

Lion, the spotted hound, died of old age. After this, Lily lost interest in going to the garden with her father, even when he introduced a new puppy to be trained. Instead, she began to take an interest in the flower garden, often helping her mother with the pruning.

Once a year, Will took the children to Wales to visit their grandfather. Widowed daughter, Annie, lived with Thomas, and the arrangement appeared successful. When Lily approached her eleventh birthday, Will and Elizabeth decided the children could take the train to Hereford, the border town, where they would be met by either Annie or Thomas in the pony cart. At the train station, Will gave instructions to lock the children in their compartment for the journey with a hamper of sandwiches and juice. They stayed several weeks in Hay, which became an annual holiday.

Will did not discuss the business or ask for any more money in the months that followed. He left for the shop after breakfast with the family, now casually dressed. Curious at what was going on, Elizabeth decided to investigate. Face well hidden behind a floppy hat, she strolled by the shop, and glanced in the small window above the door. Will was at the till, ringing up a sale. There was no sign of the Frenchman. Very much relieved at the turn of events, Elizabeth returned home.

After this, when she withdrew her semiannual one hundred pounds from her trust fund, she took a small amount for herself and deposited the rest in the business account. She presumed Will knew where the extra money was coming from, but he said nothing.

When he returned home each evening, he was genuinely tired. He spent a few minutes with her to catch up on the news of the day, played with the children, then retired to his study. She often had to knock twice on the door to call him to supper.

The following year was uneventful, allowing Elizabeth to stop worrying about everything. Lily turned twelve. Still a petite child, she was starting to show signs of maturing. She began to experiment wearing her hair in different styles, and fashion the scarves attractively. Although the scars on her neck and the puckered lip were still visible, she learned to live with them. The Dane family also became used to Lily's appearance. It was only strangers that turned their heads.

Lily had attended the exclusive academy for six years, and in the fall would move up to a higher grade along with her friends. Normally not animated, she was excited about attending the upper school, where instead of the dull uniform that juniors wore, she would wear a more attractive grown-up version. She was involved in a variety of sports, her favorite grass hockey, often played during the lunch hour, which meant she ate a sandwich at school.

Elizabeth was thinking about how well Lily had adapted to everything when George called to invite himself to lunch. Wondering his reason for an impromptu visit, she made an asparagus soup using vegetables from the garden and set a plate of cream crackers and cheese on the dining room table.

When he arrived, they went straight into the dining room for a sherry. He took a few sips then told her why he was there.

"It's an unpleasant subject I have to discuss with you, Bessie. It has come to my attention that William has been borrowing money from lenders in town and has been for some time."

Elizabeth stared at him. She reached for her glass of water, her hand shaking, spilling the water onto the linen tablecloth.

"I've spoken to the lenders involved and cleared the debt and told them to extend no more credit."

She dropped her napkin onto the damp cloth and pushed away from the table.

"Excuse me, George, I'll only be a moment. Please finish your lunch." Back straight as a rod, she hurried into the hall bathroom, and leaning her head over the basin heaved up the cream soup. She cleaned the bowl with water from the jug and using a hand towel wiped her face. When her stomach had settled, she returned to the dining room and sat down.

"I'm so sorry, Bessie, you know I'd never do anything to upset you."

"But you have."

"I had no alternative. What would you have me do?"

"I'll not have you say anything against Will. Not in this house." She picked up a cracker and nibbled it. "How much, George? How much do we owe you?"

"I didn't come for the money, Bessie. You know me better than that."

"Withdraw what we owe from the trust fund—if there is anything left."

"There is some left."

"Good. Take what we owe you."

He tilted his head and looked searchingly at her. "You'll talk to Will?"

She nodded her head. "I'll take care of it." She had no idea how.

After George left, she went upstairs to her bedroom and lay down. From what George said, there were funds to cover the loans, that's not worried her. How was she going to stop Will from taking this route? And had he used the shop as collateral for funds over and above the loans? As much as she initially put money into buying the shop, his name alone was on bank records. For all she knew she was heading into bankruptcy.

Unable to sleep she tidied her hair and returned to the dining room where she kept important papers in a small desk. The deed to the townhouse was in a folder along with other papers. The house was solely in her name having been purchased before she married. She felt sick to think she was relieved she had not added Will to the deed. She needed to talk to someone, but not George, he had never liked Will. Her bank manager was the only person she could go to for advice, someone who'd keep the discussion confidential.

When Lily arrived home from school, she found Elizabeth still sitting at the desk.

"Momma? What are you doing?" Her hair was hanging lose and her blouse untucked, and there were streaks of mud on her gym shorts.

Elizabeth replaced the folder in the desk and closed it. Usually, the desk was unlocked, but today was an unusual time. She turned the key and dropped it into her pocket.

"You go and clean up, Lily. I'll make a pitcher of lemonade and meet you in the breakfast room. I think there's still a few tea cakes left." Although the problem of how to talk to Will was not resolved, having Lily near always made her feel better.

William was restless, in and out of his study as if he didn't know what to do with himself. Freddy had gone into the playroom. Lily was sitting at the dining room table, surrounded by homework. She got up from her chair and picked something off the carpet. "What's this?" She dropped a gold cuff link onto the table.

Will examined it. The initials **GD** were engraved on the link. "Must belong to George…was he over today?"

Elizabeth had not intended to tell Will that George had come by. "He did drop in."

"And what did he want?" Will was still holding the cufflink.

"Want? He did not **want** anything, Will. He was in the neighborhood and stopped by to say hello."

Will handed Elizabeth the cuff. "When he drops by, you can give him this." He turned away and Elizabeth heard his study door open and close. She slipped the cuff link into her pocket with the desk key.

The next morning after breakfast Will said "I won't be in the shop this morning. I have some business to attend to out of town." Seeing the questioning look on Elizabeth's face, he said, "I want to buy a new gate for the garden, the old one is not keeping the pup in, she's been digging under it. She cost me a mint, I don't want to lose her or have someone entice her away."

"I gather you have someone minding the shop?"

"Part time help, always ready to make a pound or two."

After the family left, Elizabeth dressed for town. She hoped the Bank Manager, Robert Price, would see her without an appointment. She wasn't sure what she would ask him.

"Mr. Price had a cancellation if you could come back in half an hour," the clerk said. Elizabeth put in the time at a nearby teahouse, jotting a few notes as a reminder what to ask the manager.

His office door was open when she returned, and Elizabeth was immediately ushered in. Other than transferring money from her trust, Elizabeth had no reason to visit the bank. She gathered her thoughts as the manager waited. He had already welcomed her, asked how he could be of help?

"I'm not exactly sure," she said, "it's about the business, which is under my husband's name, although I am helping to pay off what remains on the loan. Could you tell me what is still owing?"

"Not a problem if you'll give me a few minutes." He went to a large metal filing cabinet, pulled out a folder, and placed it on his desk. For a moment or two he read what was written inside, jotting down a few notes. "I see you have regularly transferred funds from your trust, Mrs. Kendrick. Were you not aware that your husband renewed the loan? It stands only slightly less than the original amount." He shuffled the papers, looked uncomfortable at her silence.

"Since the business is under his name, I was not aware of any of this." She rose from her chair. "I must not take any more of your time, Mr. Price. It appears there are a few things I must discuss with my husband."

He relaxed. "If I can be of any help, you have only to ask." He extended his hand.

Elizabeth delayed returning home. She stopped at a grocery and asked them to deliver the purchases. She picked up a few items from the chemist. Her last stop was the bakery to buy a loaf of today's fresh bread, and a bag of Lily's favorite tea cakes. When she was passing the small park near the townhouse, she slipped through the gate and found a bench. She took a tea cake from the bag and ate it. She couldn't stall any more. She had to face up to having it out with Will.

She went into the house through the back door, saw the new gate propped beside the tool shed. So, William had come home, maybe left again. He was sitting in the breakfast room eating a sandwich. "I see you found what you were looking for," she said. "That should keep the pup in." She cut an end off the bread and placed the rest in the cooler. "We have to talk," she said abruptly.

"Oh? What's on your mind? You look upset."

"That's putting it mildly."

"Well, you might as well spill it out."

"I've been to the bank, had an interesting talk with Robert Price. I gather you know who Robert Price is?"

"Not really. I've dealt with several bank employees…so, what did Price have to say that's upset you? And what prompted you to go to the bank?"

"We'll leave that for a minute. I started thinking about the business loan, was curious how much is still owing?"

"Ah, so Price told you I renewed it. I was forced to, Bessie." He pushed his half-eaten sandwich away. "I told you everything was tight. Besides, what does it matter? I pay the same amount each month, just have to keep doing it a bit longer."

"That's not a good business approach, Will. What if you died tomorrow owing the bank hundreds of pounds?"

He laughed. "I don't intend to die tomorrow, but if I did you and the family would sort things out." He placed his breakfast plate in the sink. "Why do I get the feeling there is more to this discussion? You might as well get it all off your chest."

She sighed, "You couldn't be more right. It has come to my attention that you have borrowed money in town. In America these lenders are commonly known as loan sharks—a crude term, I might add."

"And if I might ask, how did you hear about this?" He ran water into the sink. "Ah, if I could be so blind? Of course, that's why George dropped by."

"It doesn't matter how I found out about the loans. I'm disgusted. Why didn't you come to me if you were strapped?"

"Bessie. Bessie. Don't you see how hard it is for me to ask you for money? Listen to your reproach. At any rate, I plan to clear the loans."

"You don't need to bother. I've taken care of them."

He returned to the table and sat down, clearly surprised, "The only thing I'm asking of you, is to add my name to the business loan. There'll be no more renewals. I'm curious, what did you need the loan money for?"

"Your spy will tell you if I don't. I had a good tip on a sporting event in Birmingham. It didn't end up so good after all. If it panned out, you would not be glaring at me."

"Obviously, you lost your money—our money. I hope you learned your lesson."

"You're a great one for lessons, Bessie. Look, I'm sorry you're distressed. The shop is slowly turning around, sales are up. What do you say we leave this discussion for another time? I'll have the bank add your name to the business account."

"Stay away from the betting," she said. "The people that run them are worse than the loan sharks."

While they sat at the table, everything between them said, Freddy arrived home from school. Elizabeth poured him a glass of milk and set a sandwich before him. Freddy attended a small private school close to the house, with primary classes lasting half days.

"Why are you home, Dada?" he said between bites of the sandwich. "Are you sick?"

"I've felt better, Freddy."

"Ask Momma for the medicine she gives me."

Under his breath, Will said, "With a dose of arsenic."

Elizabeth had heard and a smile flitted across her face. She sat back down at the table across from him. "If you're taking the gate out to the garden this afternoon, Freddy and I might join you. I haven't been there since you bought the pup."

Will looked at her, surprised. "Glad to have your company. Freddy can exercise the pup while I install the new gate. You won't mind waiting around?"

"Not at all." They were skirting each other like a couple of alley cats minus the hissing.

The garden was located a half hour from the house, and it was hard for Will and Elizabeth to keep the animosity between them going, with the sun shining, birds singing and Freddy chattering like a magpie. Will drove the cart up to the fence, dropped the reins to let the pony feed, and have water.

The garden stretched for 1/2 acre growing a variety of plants in season. The young hound, like old Lion, romped about with Freddy chasing it. Then it tired and disappeared into its doghouse.

When they arrived, Billy Sprot, the gardener, who lived in a hut on the property, was working at the far end of the field. He finished what he was doing and came over to them, all smiles when he saw Elizabeth. "So nice to see you, Mrs. Kendrick. Have you noticed the pumpkins? They'll be a good size by Guy Fawkes Day."

She followed him to the pumpkin patch while Will started installing the gate. As they were passing the hut, Billy darted in, "This was dropped off earlier." He handed Elizabeth a large brown envelope. "Looks to be a seed catalogue."

Will was finished installing the gate and had the pony hitched up ready to leave. "This came for you," she said, dropping the envelope on the seat. "Looks like a catalogue."

"You can open it," he said, "tell me what looks good."

She slit the envelope, drew out a colorful brochure. Stapled to the cover were two invoices, one for twenty-five pounds, and the other for forty-eight pounds. It was marked overdue.

When they arrived home, she picked up the bag of produce and the envelope and carried them into the house. She dropped the invoices on her desk. Turning to Will, she said, "I'll write cheques for these, and anymore that you have."

Over the months, she found many invoices needing attention on her desk. Christmas came and went, and in the first week of January, George arrived unexpectantly at the house.

He dropped his coat on the hall seat, followed by his hat and gloves. "Christmas seemed hardly the time to bring this matter up, Bessie. It's to do with your trust fund. With you constantly removing money from it, there is little left. I don't quite know what to suggest. I gather the shop is doing reasonably well. You and William must find places to cut back, live within your means. I don't imagine you want to mortgage the townhouse, your major asset."

"It's the last thing I'd do."

George picked up his belongings and started for the door. "It's a sad state of affairs you've got into, Bessie."

Lily had moved up to the higher form at the academy and had never been happier. She'd joined the school choir and a book club. She still played grass hockey and had added basketball to her sports. On this January day she had choir practice after school.

The academy was expensive, costing many pounds a year, paid from the trust fund, because Will had no means to handle this. Along with the annual cost, there were many smaller expenses. Elizabeth set aside the notebook she was using to add up figures. George's visit required great thought. She continued with her usual morning chores, then returned to her desk.

The academy fee was paid until June, the end of the term. The other expenses she could pay with housekeeping money. She wouldn't panic, and there was no need now to tell Lily that she would not be returning to the school at the end of the term. Freddy's small school fee was also paid until the summer, and other than an occasional charge for a school outing, there were no other expenses.

She tapped on the desk with her pen. Why should she and the children be the only ones to make sacrifices? Will would have to board the new hound or sell him. He'd have to lease out the garden, let Billy Sprot go. Oddly enough, this bothered her more than anything else. Such a sweet old man.

The shop had a part time employee on call. This would have to change. Will would have to return to working full time, and he would not like this.

An idea hovering at the back of her mind that she had tried to ignore surfaced. It might be the one thing to return them to a form of normalcy. Ask George to let her manage the Grande Hotel again.

There was no point contacting him now, he'd said he was going up to London. She clipped the two remaining invoices without even bothering to look at them, closed the desk.

With so much on her mind it was hard to be her usual self. Fortunately, the children were so involved in their own activities they did not notice. A week went by. She called Sophie to see if George had returned, and heard he was expected home the next day. She left a message.

When George called at the house, he said, "I knew it had to be important, Bessie, it's rare you ask to see me."

"It is rather important," she said, "and to get straight to the point, I'd like to go back to managing the hotel. You won't deny I did a good job."

"Never any doubt in my mind, but there is a problem. I've only just signed a three-year contract with a hotel group. They've done an excellent job over the last few years, and there didn't seem any reason not to renew. If I break the contract, Bessie, they'll charge a hefty fee."

"I can't change your mind?"

"I wouldn't mind doing this after a year. If you're undergoing a rough patch, I can help out."

"Thank you, George, but no. Managing the hotel was just an idea that crossed my mind." They talked about family matters, had a sherry together, and George left.

Elizabeth returned to the desk and her notebook. She crossed out 'hotel.'

She left the discussion with Will for several weeks. Then one evening when they were sitting together companionably in the parlor, she said, "How is everything going at the shop?"

"Not bad. The new clothing line is quite popular with the young people."

"I'm glad to hear that something is going well."

He frowned, shifted his feet. "What do you mean?"

"I recently discovered my trust fund is almost depleted. That means there is no money to pay for the children's private schooling. There is no money to cover the invoices you keep placing on my desk. There is no money for all our little extras."

"It also means, unless you can pay your part time employee from the proceeds of the shop, you will have to let him go and work full time yourself."

Will had straightened in the chair and was staring at her.

"If that's not enough to wake you up to our dire situation, you will have to lease out the garden, sell the hound, and find another position for Billy Sprot. At his age that will be difficult."

"Elizabeth! I can't believe you are telling me this."

"Who else can I tell, William. I'm out of options, at my wit's end."

He went to the sideboard and poured a hefty scotch, downing half in one swallow. He was holding his head as if it might fall off his shoulders.

"Sorry to spoil our pleasant evening," Elizabeth said. "I'll leave you to think everything over."

For the rest of the evening, she did not hear or see him. Before retiring she went to his study and found the door slightly open. At first, she thought the room was empty, then she saw Will slouched low in his chair, a broken glass on the floor beside him. He wasn't dead as she first thought, his breathing was shallow, almost inaudible. "Oh, dear God."

"Lucky you found him," young Dr. Macleod said, after giving Will an injection to steady his heart. "He should be checked out in a hospital. Appears he's had a heart attack."

"No hospital," she said, a replay of what she'd told the doctor when Lily had the accident. "I'll tend to him here, at home."

"I've heard that before," James Macleod said. He'd stayed on to take over old Doctor Bradley's practice. "No hospital then. Would you agree to me bringing in a specialist?"

"Of course."

William was slowly coming around. "Could we move him, upstairs to the bedroom?" Elizabeth asked.

"I'm not sure if that's a good idea, yet. Fetch a blanket to keep him warm, and I'll push the stool under his feet. His pulse is regular, and his breathing normal. I think it best he stays put. He'll likely sleep."

Elizabeth walked to the door with the doctor. "How is young Lily doing," he asked before leaving. "She must be twelve, thirteen?"

"Thirteenth birthday soon. And she's wonderful. I always hoped her lip would improve, but it hasn't. The scars on her neck are about the same."

"Yes. Today I might have done something different with treating the burns, but what's done is done. I've heard physicians in Europe are experimenting with skin grafts. Perhaps she can take advantage of this."

Leaving the study door open, Elizabeth went into the kitchen to make herself tea. She was physically and emotionally drained. No doubt giving Will the alternatives had brought on the heart attack.

"Momma? Is Dada going to be all right?"

"I believe so, Lily. He'll need to take it easy for a while. Would you like to go and sit with him while I have my tea?"

"I'll hold his hand, Momma, so he knows I'm there. It will comfort him."

In the morning, with the banister on one side, Elizabeth on the other, and Lily behind, Will climbed the stairs to the bedroom. He was weak and paused several times before getting into bed. "Lily will stay with you while I take care of few chores," Elizabeth said. "For one, I'm going over to the shop to close it for the day. I'll be back shortly."

She placed a sign in the window, purchased a few items in town and returned home. Will was sleeping. "The doctor came by, Momma, and he left Dada an envelope of pills." Lily pointed to the table. "He said to tell you he's arranged for another doctor to examine Dada, and he'll let you know when."

"Elizabeth took Lily by the arm. Your father looks peaceful. Come, I want to talk to you about my plan." This had come to her while printing out the note to close the shop for the day. "When Freddy has left for school, I'll get Maggie to stay here with your father. Then I'll open the shop. And I'll ask the other tailor in town to handle our orders, so we don't lose the business. That's where you come in."

Lily's eyes widened. "Me?"

"You're very bright, Lily. I'll show you how to work the till. You can come right after school, let me go home."

"But I'm not even thirteen, Momma. And what about basketball practice?"

"Keeping everything running smoothly is more important than basketball. And if you were living in Wales, you'd already be working."

Lily said nothing.

"The shop is carrying a new line of clothing for younger men. Perhaps having a young person show them the clothing might induce them to make a purchase?"

"How long do I have to do this?"

"Until your father is back on his feet."

Since the weekend was approaching, Elizabeth did not set the plan in motion until Monday. She took an hour on Sunday to show Lily how to write up an order and handle the cash register. They went through the various items such as the tie rack and boxes of socks.

"Ties and socks could be put together, Momma. Like, coordinate them."

"What a good idea. That'll give you a project while you're waiting for a customer."

The heart specialist came to the house and examined Will. He normally did not make house calls, but James had convinced him to make an exception. The diagnosis was correct. Will had suffered a mild heart attack. Elizabeth was asked to keep Will quiet, and free of stress. He would be his usual self in two to three weeks.

"And no alcohol," said the doctor.

It took Elizabeth a few days to get into the routine. Asking the town's other tailor to take any orders that came in and letting the part-time employee know for the time being there would be no call for work, were the first things Elizabeth did. She hadn't done anything about Billy Sprot and the garden, or the hound.

Toward the end of the first week Will put on a robe and spent part of the day in a chair in the bedroom. When she came into the room, he was sitting with a shaving kit in front of him. Refusing to let Maggie help, he had nicked himself in several places. She set the shaving kit aside and placed a tray with a coffee and a tea on the table. "How are you feeling?"

"Worse than being trampled on the field."

She added sugar and cream to his coffee. "I've been feeling a good share of guilt, dropping the load on you all at once."

"It wouldn't have mattered if I'd been hit then or later. You've closed the shop, I expect?"

She smiled. "Not at all. I've been working hard at making sales, I received two orders for suits today. And your daughter, bless her soul, has had equal success. She's rearranged the smaller items, placing a few in the window to draw in customers."

"Lily agreed to help in the shop?"

Elizabeth laughed, "Only after I informed her if she was in Wales, she'd be working in the coal mine."

"I think you have to be fourteen," he said, with his first show of humor.

"Whatever. She doesn't mind. Ask her when she gets home."

"At any rate, the most important thing is for you to get better. I've left off talking to Billy for now. Maybe we can work something out." She bent over and kissed him gently. "I'll be back up shortly."

As they moved into the second week, Will got bored. Elizabeth suggested Freddy play checkers or any card game with his father to break the routine. Lily began spending time with him, relating events of the shop. Will noticeably brightened after the visits with the children.

During the third week, Will spent the day downstairs, alternating his time between the kitchen and the parlor. Other than talking about what was happening at the shop, Elizabeth stayed away from any mention of finances. At the end of the third week, James Macleod came to the house.

"You're all set to resume your daily routine," he said, "but, William, do lay back on the drinking. If you must, keep it to one a day."

Lily's birthday was celebrated with a family dinner at the hotel. She had styled her hair in a becoming way and wore a new dress of mauve shot silk. At her neck, she had twined a scarf of the same colors, and wore silver earrings in her newly punctured ears. She still helped at the shop and had suggested she continue. "I was never that good at basketball, Momma. You have to be tall."

"Then concentrate at what you are good at, Lily, like the piano. It's gathering dust."

Elizabeth had avoided thinking about the future of the children's schooling, particularly Lily's. End of school term would soon arrive. Lily would have to leave the academy and enroll at the public school three blocks way. The subject was difficult to approach. On the first of June, the academy sent a letter stating particulars for enrollment in September, including the fee, which had increased. The time had come to talk to Lily.

After the letter came, on the Sunday afternoon, Elizabeth suggested she and Lily visit The Commandery, many times restored hospital, dating back to the 1000s, more recently owned by the City of Worcester. Walkways and courtyards surrounded the main building and were favorite places for families to stroll. Elizabeth had visited numerous times, but Lily had not. Will drove them to the area and agreed to pick them up later outside the Great Hall.

After spending some time looking around, they found a bench close to where Will and Freddy would meet them. Elizabeth set aside the brochure she was reading and turned her attention to Lily. "There is something I have to talk to you about, and I have put off doing so. You know that your father's shop has struggled the last while—although it is doing better now—but we are forced to cut back on expenses. I've avoided telling you this, but you will **not** be returning to the academy in September, you will attend Crossroads Public School in town."

Without a word, Lily stood up, and walked toward the entrance of the site. Elizabeth caught up with her. "If there was any other way, I'd take it."

"I don't want to talk about it, Momma. Look! There's Dada and Freddy." Several days passed with no mention of school. Then in the middle of August, Lily said, "I walked by Crossroads. The doors were open. When do I register?"

"I'll look into this," said Elizabeth.

"You don't have to do anything, Momma. I'm old enough to register myself."

A day later, Lily placed an envelope on the kitchen table. "I'm now officially enrolled in Crossroads Middle School—at least after you sign your name on the form." She took a banana from the bowl on the table and began to peel it. "What about Freddy? Is he changing schools, too?" She dropped the peeling in the garbage container under the sink.

The fee for Freddy's school was much smaller than Lily's, and it could be paid by installments. After much thought, Elizabeth had paid for Freddy up to Christmas. "For now, he'll continue at the same school."

End of subject.

Lily was staring at her face in the hall mirror. She was dressed for the first day at the new school in a two-piece plaid skirt and blouse, her long hair tied back with a green ribbon. She had tucked a green scarf into the neck of the blouse. Turning away from the mirror, she said, "I expect everyone will look at me."

"That's only because you're a new girl."

Lily shrugged her shoulders, "I'm used to it."

A few weeks later Lily came home from school and went directly to the piano. She pulled out sheets of music from inside the bench. When she saw Elizabeth watching, she said, "The choir is practicing for a Christmas concert. They need someone to play the piano during intermission. I thought I'd volunteer—if no one else does."

Elizabeth was careful not to show too much enthusiasm. She wanted Lily to get used to the school and fitting in. "You play well," she said. "Do we have the kind of music you are looking for?"

"I think so." She set sheets of music on the piano and began to play. A few days later while having their tea, she said, "No one else volunteered, so I did. Would you help me choose the pieces I will play?" She paused, "Would you like to come to the concert, Momma?"

Elizabeth picked up a sheet of music. "Of course. I'll ask your father to come, too."

William tried hard to change his life. He did not complain about putting in long hours at the shop, and he worked on Sundays in the walled garden. They came to a compromise with Billy Sprot, the gardener, who continued to live in the hut on the property and act as caretaker. Unfortunately, Will had to sell the hound. Best of all, he had cut back on his drinking, or so it seemed. Elizabeth suspected that at some point of his day, he dropped into a pub.

He regularly gave her housekeeping money, enough that she could put a little aside to pay for Freddy's school activities. Will also gave Lily a small amount of cash for helping in the shop. The months moved on into the new year without any disruptions. Elizabeth began to breathe easier.

Then, in the spring of 1909, a messenger on a bicycle, rang the townhouse bell, breathless. He handed Elizabeth a note from the proprietor of the Happy Stag, a pub situated in the shabbier part of town. Will had collapsed, was now resting in one of the pub's back rooms. A doctor had seen to him. She dropped a few coins in the messenger's hand, grabbed her coat, and found transportation to the pub. The courtyard was deserted. Barrels of trash and empty bottles were stacked against a side wall. The entrance needed sweeping. Why was Will in a place like this?

She soon found out. A round table at the back of the pub was occupied by three men, one of them Johnny, Will's rugby friend. Mugs of ale, some half empty, were scattered about the table, along with a platter of half-eaten cheese. Johnny jumped from the chair and before she could say anything, he grabbed her arm. "You made it quick, Ma'am."

"What's going on?"

"Nothing much, just having a bit of a gab." He pointed to the back of the pub. "Will's stretched out there."

She pushed him aside, and entered the snug, a small room set aside for ladies who wanted to drink discreetly. Will was sitting up, apparently recovered. She grabbed his arm. "What are you doing in this dreadful place? Never mind answering, you can tell me when we get home."

She helped him upstairs to the bedroom. "We'll talk after the children have gone to bed." She firmly shut the door.

"So, a doctor looked you over? What did he say?" She was back in their bedroom.

"Said I was all right, had a bit too much of the good stuff," he laughed. "Cheap ale never agreed with me."

"You could have picked a classier place to meet your cronies. Have you been there before?"

"A few times. That's where the boys stay when they're in town."

"I see."

"No, you don't. It's all work and no play for you, my dear Bessie."

"Is someone tending the shop?" she glanced at her watch. "It is only four o'clock."

"Someone's looking after it."

"I hope they're reliable, not stealing you blind."

He shut his eyes, a way to ignore her. She closed the bedroom door and returned to the parlor. That night she slept in the guest room.

She rose later than usual the next morning. Lily and Freddy were finishing breakfast. There was no sign of Will. "Have you seen your father?" she asked Lily.

Lily stared at her breakfast cereal. "He was going out the door when I got up. Did you quarrel, Momma?"

"Nothing serious, just a little spat." She picked up the breakfast dishes and set them in the sink. Will arrived home that evening at the usual time, and nothing more was said about the earlier episode.

Lily finished her school year with much less fanfare than at the academy. She did, however, receive glowing reports from her teachers, especially the music teacher. She had turned fourteen and was becoming a little lady.

Freddy, at twelve, was still more concerned with playing ball, and Elizabeth hoped this was not a sign he was following in his father's footsteps. It was decided the children would spend the summer in Hay with Thomas and Annie, both getting on in years. Elizabeth and Will saw them on to the train, returning home to an empty house.

They sat across from each other at the dining room table. As a treat, Elizabeth had poured them goblets of wine. Will was not overly fond of wine, much preferring whiskey, or brandy. He took a small sip, put his glass down. His hand trembled, not for the first time, she recalled.

Without being obvious, she watched him eat his dinner, how he handled his knife and fork. It wasn't until she served him a bowl of ice cream and fruit, that the tremble reoccurred. She decided to say nothing at this time but would watch in the days ahead.

Summer was a quiet time at the shop, and Will decided to close the store on Monday's. At first, he stayed around the house doing small chores, then as the summer moved along and he became bored, he left the house following lunch. Elizabeth did not ask where he was going, had decided she could not be his keeper. He was always home to have dinner with her.

It was in the middle of August when she had an unexpected visit from George. Because of the feelings between the two men, she had not seen much of her brother.

She glanced at the hall clock, close to five. Will would be home shortly.

Elizabeth ushered George into the parlor and poured them sherries. "A pleasant surprise," she said.

"May not be," he said. "I always seem to be the bearer of bad news, Bessie."

"Oh? And what have you brought me today?"

"I'm perplexed. I stopped at the feed store to pick up a bag of oats to drop off at the stables. You know that's where I board Lady?"

"And?"

It was unusual for George to be at a loss for words. "It's a part of town I usually avoid. That pub, the Happy Stag, next door invites a bad crowd. You likely don't know of it."

"I've heard of it." Elizabeth held her breath, knowing what was coming next.

"Anyway, I was loading the oats into the buggy when a rowdy group fell out of the pub. All backslapping, laughing. And who is with them? William."

"What can I say?"

"Bessie, we've had these discussions before. Your Will is cheapening the family name. It's bad enough to almost go bankrupt, but to be carousing around like what I saw today is despicable. You talk to him again and again about changing his ways, but you are far too soft with him. This Welshman has you wrapped around his little finger." He stood up, "I've had my say, so must leave, and talk this over with your brothers."

"Before you go, George, there's something I want to say. From the first day I brought William to your home, you have shown your dislike. You never saw the good in him, only the bad. I know he's not perfect—none of us are, including you."

"Now, now, Bessie, be fair, I did offer to help set him up."

"At the cost of him losing his independence. But as the saying goes, that's water under the bridge. I don't want to quarrel with you, George, or with any of my brothers. I will talk to him, I expect he was at the pub visiting with his old pal, Johnny. Far as I gather, none of them play rugby anymore, age has caught up with them. And I do agree they should look for a more respectable place to meet." She saw George to the door.

Will arrived home shortly after. Before he'd hung up his jacket, he said, "From the look on your face, you've got bad news for me. So, let's have it."

"George came by. He saw you and your pals leaving the pub."

"Has he started to follow me?" he said with a quizzical look.

"Of course not! He had a legitimate reason for being in the area. It was your behavior he was questioning."

"I can see mealy-mouth George would do that."

"I'm not against you meeting your friends, Will, it's the place you choose to do so, and how you deport yourselves. Besides, after the last episode there, I thought you'd learned your lesson."

He grabbed his jacket. "I've had enough of your lessons tonight, Bessie. I'm going out for some air." He returned well after the dinner hour and went directly to his study where he stayed until morning when he joined her at the breakfast table.

"I've decided to go home for a visit with Da and Annie and will bring the children back with me. I'll ask my man at the shop to stay on for a bit, then leave directly. Give you time to cool off."

"Just as you like."

A day or two after he left, Elizabeth went to the shop. There was a sign on the door stating the business was open Tuesday to Friday. No one was around, and the front door was locked.

Will arrived back with the children in time for them to enroll in the new school year. He was in a jovial mood. "I gather you had a good visit with the family," she said when they were eating dinner the first night back.

"That I did."

She glanced at the children, Lily with a sprinkle of freckles across the bridge of her nose, both children tanned from days under the Welsh sun. "I'm glad." After the children left the table, she said, "I dislike bringing up business so soon after you've arrived home, but I think you'd better go by the shop. Did you plan to change the hours while you were away?"

He frowned, "I did mention an old employee was looking after everything."

Several weeks passed. The children started school, Lily joined the choir, and Freddy took a sudden interest in the school's chess club, which brought great relief to Elizabeth. She backed off discussing the shop with Will. They were getting along reasonably well, and he was unusually quiet. She wondered if he was ill.

She heard no more from the George Dane family until early December when Sophie invited her and the children to a matinee. They were seated in a tea house following the performance, when Sophie, making small talk said, "What do you think of this Suffragette movement in London? I'm not sure I agree with them."

It had been years since Elizabeth visited London. Occasionally a brother would come home for a visit. Brother James and his wife Gladys had emigrated to Canada. She heard from them at Christmas. Another brother had left for America. Unfortunately, he drowned shortly after acquiring property, an apple orchard she recalled.

"I don't know a lot about the suffragettes, but I do believe women should stand up for their rights." The talk drifted off to other matters.

"How is the business doing?" Sophie asked after a bit. "And William?"

She carefully answered, doubting George had confided in Sophie about William, but one never knows. "It has its ups and downs like most businesses." She changed the subject.

The festive season came and went, and the new year, 1911, arrived with little fanfare. Lily was approaching her fifteenth birthday. She insisted on wearing white gloves, and often a hat when she accompanied Elizabeth to town. Freddy had graduated to long trousers, in every way a little gentleman. He rarely went on the mother and daughter outings.

Then, one spring day Will arrived home from the shop early. Instead of going into his study, he went into the kitchen where Elizabeth was starting dinner. He poured himself a drink of water. "I had a funny spell," he said to her enquiring look.

"Do I need to call the doctor?"

"I'll sit for a while. It'll likely pass." He leaned his head back against the cushions in the breakfast nook and closed his eyes. She watched him for a minute. "I'll make us tea," she said, filling the kettle.

He shook his head, "Not for me, thanks. I'm going to lie down."

"All right. If you're not better, I'll send for Dr. Macleod." When she looked in later, Will was sleeping. He was very pale, and there was a sheen of moisture on his forehead. Better safe than sorry, she thought as she sent a message off to the doctor.

He had examined Will and was standing with Elizabeth outside the bedroom door. "It's a warning, Mrs. Kendrick. A small stroke. William will be fine in a day or so, but he could have another. Have you noticed any changes in his health?"

"A few months ago, I noticed his hand trembling, nothing recently. How serious is a small stroke?"

"It's common, often followed by another. More severe ones cause damage to the limbs. There's no sign of anything like this with William."

She walked with him to the stairs. "I'll watch for changes." They descended to the main floor. "Thank you for coming, Doctor, and good night."

She stood for a moment in the hall, thinking. She had to tell Will about the stroke. He was approaching his forty-ninth birthday. If ever there was a time to change his habits, it was now. She called out to Lily. "Your father is not well. Please sit with him while I make a cool drink. You can tell him about your music program, that will interest him."

When she returned with a lemonade, Lily slipped out of the room. Elizabeth sat on the edge of the bed. She took Will's hand. "I'm going to be completely truthful with you. Dr. Macleod thinks you have had a small stroke." Panic crossed his face, startling her. He knew, as most people, that a stroke could mean loss of function of arms and legs, or death.

"It was not severe, a day or so you'll feel fine. It means, though, you must make changes in your routine and habits. I haven't thought everything out, but I'll do whatever is necessary to help, the children, too."

"I'm done for," he said bluntly, with a shake of his head.

"Nonsense! You've years of good health left if you're sensible." She handed him the lemonade. "Where's the cocky Welshman who courted me? I want to see him back." She got a small smile from him. "I'll give the children their dinner, then we can talk."

When she returned to the bedroom he was standing before the mirror dressed in pajamas and a robe. "As handsome as ever," she said. "Let's sit on the couch and talk."

"The shop is the first matter of importance," she began. "School will be out in a week for the summer. Between you and Lily you can keep the shop going. I'll help, as well. I'm sure Billy Sprot will agree to work the garden during the summer growing season. Let's take it one step at a time."

"You've always been more organized than me, Bessie. Expect you inherited it. I was better running down the field kicking the ball, shouting to the lads. All finished, just like me."

"Tonight, you feel down, everything will look better tomorrow."

"I hope so."

The summer moved along. Freddy started working in the back of the shop a few hours a week unpacking boxes, stacking empty ones, sweeping up. As back up for Will, Lily was more than competent in the front. Despite all of this, sales dropped. It was as if the town was not convinced that the business was solid.

They were having an early Sunday tea, when Lily announced, she was not returning to school. "I shall stay helping Dada in the shop, actually, I've come to like it." She had been out earlier in the day and had not changed from a skirt and blouse, with the usual scarf tucked into the neck. Standing before Elizabeth was a young lady, no longer a child.

"I'd like you to stay in school until you are fifteen, Lily. That's still five months away."

She looked thoughtful. "What if I went half days. I could work in the shop afternoons." Up until then, Elizabeth and Will alternated hours in the shop, and to cut back on expenses, they had cancelled their accountant. Elizabeth was now managing the books, quite accomplished at this from her years running the hotel.

"I'll talk to them at school," Lily said, "See what they say."

It was Elizabeth's day at the shop, and it was quiet. She had set out the business books on the long table used to measure fabric when the bell on the door tinkled and George walked in. Instead of feeling pleased to see him, she felt a sense of dread. "Are you alone?" he asked.

She glanced around at the empty shop. "Unless someone is hiding under the counter, I am alone. What brings you here, George?"

"I've given your circumstances much thought lately—an ailing husband, a declining business to mention only a few things. So, I have a suggestion."

"And what might that be? Have I suddenly come into a vast inheritance?"

"Unfortunately, no. My suggestion is you and the family leave Evesham and emigrate to either Australia or Canada."

She was so shocked she was speechless. "At forty-eight years of age?"

"I know you're not as young as most emigrants, but you still have lots of good years ahead—working years in a new environment."

"I can't believe you want me to leave my home, my town, to get rid of me."

"Don't put it that way, Bessie."

"How else can I put it?"

"I will never go to Australia."

"But in Canada, you'd have family. I'm trying to do what's best for you, Bessie. Make a new start—opportunities for the children. If you're not happy there, you can always return."

"How considerate."

He blinked at the sarcasm in her voice.

"Well, I'll leave you to think about it."

After George left, Elizabeth was too upset to continue working on the accounts. She hung the Closed sign on the door, locked up and returned home.

She was sitting in the kitchen drinking a cup of tea when Lily walked in. "You're home early, Momma, is something wrong?"

"I suppose there is. Your uncle George upset me," she hesitated, wondering how much to tell Lily. "He said that we should leave the area, emigrate someplace, likely Canada."

Lily placed her packages down. "Why would he suggest that?"

Lily was not blind to the negative feelings between George and Will, or conditions in the house. "George cannot bear to have your father here, and of course he knows I'd never leave your father."

"We studied Canada at school, I told the class I had relatives there. Are you going to tell Dada?"

"I don't see any way around not telling him."

Lily picked up her packages. "He might like the idea. He doesn't do anything here."

Elizabeth waited for the right time to approach Will. She did not know what to expect. He surprised her by saying, "Two of my mates emigrated and got free land, became farmers. So, old George is trying to get rid of me? Why am I not surprised? At least in Canada I wouldn't have to look at his face." They were sitting in his study. He'd poured himself a drink from the decanter and returned to his chair. No more was said.

Elizabeth made small enquiries about the immigration process. She found that her baker had a brother who'd moved to Canada, and Maggie, the housemaid, had an uncle living there. She began to feel more comfortable with the idea.

Lily brought home books and a map of Canada and asked her mother to look at them. Freddy thought the whole idea was exciting. Will asked Lily if her mother had any more thoughts on the idea. Gradually, over the months, the idea took hold. "I'll go to the immigration office with you, Momma," said Lily.

Elizabeth nodded. Her grownup daughter had a good head on her shoulders. Whatever would she do without Lily?

It took several tries to find the location of the immigration office, several towns away. Elizabeth finally got an appointment for the middle of November, surely the coolest, dampest time of the year. She kept Will informed of their plans, but after the first day he showed little interest.

Elizabeth and Lily dressed warmly for the coach ride, and overnight stay at the hotel, a short walk to the government office. Lily carried the folder with the family particulars. She was unusually quiet, obviously nervous.

They sat in a dreary office waiting for their name to be called. Finally, they were directed into an inner room lined with shelves full of papers and books. Both Elizabeth and Lily had taken care in their dress, and despite wearing bulky clothes to ward off the cold, they managed to look stylish.

After the introductions were over, the immigration officer, Mr. Stocker, started the interview by asking Elizabeth why she wanted to emigrate to Canada. This was followed by several questions about their knowledge of the new country and what they planned to do when they arrived.

"And your husband, Ma'am, does he share your same interest in Canada? You have a teenage son, I believe?"

Elizabeth hesitated, not sure how much to disclose about Will's health. "My husband is not with us today because we own a clothing business. And, of course, my thirteen-year-old son is at school."

More questions followed, then the officer introduced the matter of Elizabeth and Will's age. "Most emigrants are much younger than you. Youth is always on the side of applying, always taken into consideration. You are in good health?"

"Excellent. And you can see my daughter is also in good health, as is my son. My intention is when we arrive in Canada, we will find employment. My son, Frederick, will be fifteen in two years' time, finished his schooling, and will work also." She shifted in her chair and wiped a bead of perspiration from her forehead.

"Shall I get you a glass of water, Momma?" Lily asked, noting her mother's discomfort.

Officer Stocker pointed to a water dispenser and waited until Lily was again seated. "And your husband, what is the condition of his health?"

Elizabeth took a long sip of the water. How truthful should she be? "My husband had a mild heart attack some years ago. He fully recovered." She made no mention of the stroke. "We have more than enough funds to get established in the new country from the sale of the business and our townhouse. We do not require any government help or charity." She walked to the water dispenser and set the glass firmly down.

A small smile flittered across the officer's face. "That's all we need to cover today, Mrs. Kendrick. The office will communicate with you before the New Year. Thank you for coming in and good day to both of you." He walked them to the door.

When they were back at the hotel having tea, Lily said, "How do you think the interview went, Momma?"

"I'm not sure. I haven't a lot of experience with occasions like that."

Lily finished her tea biscuit. "You handled the questions well, especially when Mr. Stocker asked about Dada's health. And when you said we were not asking for charity."

"Thank you, Lily, you were a great support. Well, we'll see what develops." She glanced at the street, "Too cold to do anything but sit by the fire. I'll stay in the lobby until dinner time. You do whatever you like." She sat thinking about the interview, not sure if she wanted their applications accepted or not. Time would tell.

While away, Elizabeth had arranged for Maggie to make dinner for Will and Freddy. When she arrived home the next day, all was well. Will, neatly dressed, was sitting before the fire in the parlor. "How did it go?" he asked.

"All right, I suppose. It's hard to know. The office will be in touch by the new year."

"So, we don't know if I'm to take up trout fishing or not?"

"Sorry. You may have to put your energies into an activity here."

At the end of December, she had a brief letter from immigration. Her application had gone to another department for review. This did not sound promising. However, through the bank, she began to make enquiries about finding a buyer for the shop. And she spoke with an agent about selling the townhouse. On New Year's Eve the bank called to say they had an offer on the clothing business. An appointment was set for the second week of January. There was still no word from immigration.

Every day Lily asked if she'd heard? "Stop pestering me," Elizabeth said. "I'll tell you one way or another as soon as I hear."

She and Lily spent every day in the shop tidying the stock. Will accompanied them most days but he seemed to have lost interest. It would be good to be free of the business no matter what happened, she decided.

She went alone for the appointment with the prospective buyer, and with a bank employee by her side, she signed the paper on behalf of Will. After the final accounting, a reasonable amount remained to go toward a new purchase, hopefully, in Canada.

Elizabeth was getting as jittery as Lily, waiting each day for the mail, often meeting the postman before he got to the door. When the large brown envelope finally arrived, she was afraid to open it. She was alone in the house having convinced Will and Lily to walk into town for a few purchases. Freddy was at school.

She placed the large envelope on the dining room table, thinking, surely it did not require such a bulky package to tell them their application was denied? She slit the paper. A letter was attached to several forms, along with brochures. She carried the letter over to her desk to read.

The application had been based on the fact she had two working age children. Smiling to herself, Freddy was hardly old enough to work. There was no mention of a husband. She reread the letter to ensure Will was included in the application.

The next part of the letter informed them space in Second Class was available on one of two ships leaving Liverpool, destination Halifax, Nova Scotia, Canada, either May 25th, 1912, or June 15th, 1912. Her hand shook badly, she dropped the letter onto the desk. It all seemed too real. She was sitting at the desk when the family arrived home.

Lily took the purchases into the kitchen and returned to the dining room. "You're pale, Momma. Are you alright?"

Elizabeth covered the letter with her hand. "I've heard from immigration."

"Oh, no! They've denied our application. Why? Can we resubmit?" A tear rolled down her cheek.

"Let me finish, Lily. I heard from immigration to say they had accepted our application. But I am having second thoughts. I cannot leave England like a refugee, wander off in the wilderness as they did in the bible. I absolutely cannot!"

Will had pulled a chair over to the desk. Lily was staring at her, the tears drying. "You can't turn it down, Momma. Do you want them to think we don't know our own minds?"

"People surely change their minds all the time. The immigration office is likely used to it."

"Please, Momma, let me read the letter. You're always telling me not to be hasty."

Elizabeth pushed the envelope over. "Just as you like."

The following morning, Lily said, "I talked to Dada, Momma. He'll be glad to leave, the town has not been good to him. I want to leave, too, Momma. Canada is a huge, open country. We'll be happy there." She sipped her hot chocolate. "I read everything in the envelope. We must start right away with the forms. We need to confirm our bookings. We need to send money for the passage." She took her mother's hand. "Please, Momma. Don't change your mind."

"I want to take the day to think this through," said Elizabeth. "I'll make up my mind by dinner." She closed the door to the dining room to discourage interruptions and sat back at her desk. They had less than four months to meet the immigration schedule. The townhouse and contents still had to be sold. She needed to investigate employment opportunities in British Columbia, the province they had decided on, get references from the bank. She could not rely on Will for help, but dear, sweet Lily would be there for her all the way.

Thinking about Lily made her pause. The child—not a child anymore—but a young lady approaching her sixteenth birthday, from the day she was born had never complained about anything. She had made the best of her imperfections, had agreeably helped cut down on expenses, like changing schools, dropping music and dancing lessons, and more recently, taken on the responsibility of the shop. Where could a mother ever find a more perfect daughter? Up until now Lily had not asked for anything. Now she wanted a new life with adventure. Who else but a mother could provide for this?

Rather than wait until dinner, Elizabeth set out a special tea in the dining room at four o'clock. She called in the family. She poured the tea and passed the small cakes and said, "I expect you have been waiting with bated breath for my decision. I'm not totally sure if I'm doing the right thing, but we'll carry on with our original plans. And if emigrating proves wrong, I have only myself to blame." She looked at the family, it was as if they'd been holding their breath.

The days flew by in a flurry of activity. Lily helped Elizabeth write the letter to immigration to confirm the arrangements, and they attached a bank draft to cover their fares. Elizabeth prodded the agent to find a buyer for the townhouse and was relieved when he did.

The family began to select items to take with them. They had decided on one steamer trunk each and another for household items. The dining room table was piled high with silverware, two linen tablecloths with matching napkins, and household items.

When she added a few valuable ornaments to the trunk, Elizabeth said with a sad smile, "We can always sell them if necessary." Books were too heavy to pack, but Lily slipped in a few favorites without her mother's knowledge, as did Freddy.

Will packed his own trunk, filling it with rugby trophies, his captain's shield, and a baton from his time in the militia. Elizabeth looked at his half-filled trunk. "Let's include your mother's embroidery and your father's weaving," she suggested, handing him a package.

George came by in late March. Elizabeth had already told Sophie their plans. George stayed in the hall, didn't remove his coat and had little to say. When he left, Elizabeth found an envelope on the table with a bank draft for fifty pounds inside. Alan came from London to say goodbye, bringing good wishes from Charles and Wallace who were tending to the business. Their cards included sums of money. Albert, the second oldest brother, and wife, Christina, were in India, and Elizabeth doubted they'd never meet again. This caused her to reflect on the enormity of their undertaking.

Several communications from immigration arrived—their tickets would be waiting for them at the Railway Hotel where they would stay one or two nights before boarding. The government offered relocation funds to help with their expenses. They had to apply. Elizabeth was not going to bother but Lily said it was foolish to turn down good money. She filled out the request and had Elizabeth sign it.

Surprisingly, before going to the province of British Columbia, immigration required them to make a six-week stop at a farm community near Brandon, Manitoba, staying with a family who would help them familiarize with Canada.

Once a week Elizabeth bought a London newspaper to keep up with world affairs. This week a special section showed a picture of the Titanic with pennants and flags flying in the breeze. The ship had completed its sea trials in Ireland and was ready to take on passengers in Southampton for its maiden voyage across the Atlantic arriving in New York on April 10. For all accounts, it was far more luxurious than the ship they'd be on six weeks later. Elizabeth left the paper for Lily to look at.

The days moved ahead. Lily celebrated her 16th birthday on March 13th, but on the 7th, her actual birthday, her mother baked a mini cake and set it before her at dinner that night.

A letter from immigration confirmed they would be travelling aboard the Carthaginian on May 25th, with two weeks at sea.

Each day the family added small items to their trunk—six soldered soldiers and a train set for Freddy, and a bag of marbles. Lily placed sheet music, a small jewel case that held her combs and her glass-eyed, china baby doll in her trunk. Elizabeth had set aside several articles to choose from, finally deciding on a cut-glass vinegar bottle, salts, and a favorite cup and saucer. Will tried to fit into his trunk a carved cane that he no longer used but gave up when he could not make it fit.

The family was busy, invited for goodbye lunches and dinners. Instead of a dinner at her home, Sophie invited Elizabeth and Lily for lunch at the Grande Hotel. It was an intimate lunch with only the three of them since she knew Elizabeth was on uncertain terms with George. When they were leaving the hotel, she presented Elizabeth with a paisley scarf and kid gloves. She had rolled up the hotel's New Year's Menu for a souvenir. She gave Lily a box of silk scarves in various designs, and mother of pearl hair combs. Sophie and George were leaving for France and would be away when Elizabeth and family departed.

There was little to do now that the trunks were packed and placed in the hall. It was early April, and the weather was balmy. Will had taken the trap and gone to the garden to say goodbye to old Billy Sprot who had decided to move into town to a funded home for the aged. Without William knowing, Elizabeth had given Billy twenty pounds to make his life easier. He would stay on at the garden until they left, be there to show the new owners the ins and outs of the place. Will would likely drop in at a pub on his way home, but she didn't mind since there would be few occasions ahead.

Holding a pencil to mark their route, Elizabeth was studying the map of Canada that Lily had spread out on the dining room table, forcing them to eat their meals in the kitchen, when she heard the Town Cryer, keeping with tradition, belting out the news. **"Titanic. Titanic Sinks in Atlantic**."

She dropped the pencil and rushed into the street. The Town Cryer had turned in to the next lane. Back inside the house, she grabbed her coat and started for town. The news of a ship sinking did not mean a lot to most people, many ships went down over the years. She rushed into the hotel where they were sure to have more news. The desk clerk said, "It's a gruesome affair with all those bodies floating about. I'll keep my traveling close to home, no ships for me."

"How many were lost?"

"Hundreds. Thousands or more I've heard. Hit an iceberg." He turned back to the register. Elizabeth took a chair by the window. The news had made her ill. If they were not traveling the same route, in the same manner, the news would have been sad, but not shocking. She continued to sit by the window until the clerk's glances forced her to leave.

Back at the house she could not get the picture of the magnificent ship going to the bottom of the sea. When Lily returned from her walk, she found her mother sitting in the parlor staring at nothing.

"What's wrong, Momma?" She slipped into a chair across from her Elizabeth.

"I've heard the most unbelievable, shocking news. The Titanic has gone down."

"Gone down? What do you mean?"

"Sank. I feel quite sick, Lily."

Lily had been fascinated with the new ship and had collected the pictures from the London paper showing the various stages of the ship being built. Now, she brought them from her bedroom and laid them on the table, stared at them for several minutes, then returned them to their envelope.

Elizabeth could not get the news of the sinking out of her mind. It was like having an abscess tooth that needed attention. The trunks lined up in the hall were bad omens. For several days she did nothing toward their departure, until Lily said, "Momma, we've still got six weeks before we leave, why don't we go over to Hay and visit Annie?"

It was like grasping at a straw. "Yes. A good idea. The visit will get my mind off this other news."

They took an overnight coach into the town, where they had booked a one-night stay at the Lion Hotel. Elizabeth had not seen any of the family for years. After Thomas died, Will lost track of his brothers and sisters. When they arrived at the cottage at the top of the hill, other than a new coat of paint on the steps, everything looked the same. They knocked, then banged at the door, no one answered. Freddy climbed onto a stoop to look in the window. "Table is set," he called back. They were about to leave when a shout came from the street.

Henry, Will's younger brother, loped up the path. "Look who's here," he called out. He unlocked the door, ushered them in. He'd taken over the cottage when he got laid off at the mine. Annie had moved into town to subsidized housing.

Henry ladled Will a shot of home brew still in the crock, while Elizabeth made herself tea. They visited a short while, catching up on family news, then walked back into town, found the row-house Annie lived in and visited with her in the garden. She could not understand why anyone wanted to leave their home when she'd never been more than a few miles from hers.

They had dinner together at the hotel, and the next morning the family caught the day coach back home. The visit was not overly satisfying but it did get Elizabeth's mind off the tragedy of the past week. The family finished their packing and other preparations for leaving Evesham.

Part 2

The children were wide-eyed at the throngs of people at the Liverpool station. After travelling several hours from Evesham, they'd stepped down from the train and joined the masses. Lily and Freddy found their trunks in a different compartment, set them against a wall and waited for their parents to catch up. It was too far to walk to the Railway Hotel, where they had two nights reserved. Elizabeth sent the children to find a cart and handler to lift the trunks in behind a tired horse.

At the hotel, Elizabeth said, "I'll book us in." She clutched their precious documents folded into a portmanteau. When she pushed open the hotel door and entered the lobby, it was as if she'd stepped back in time to another hotel, in another place. The strange sensation disappeared as she moved to the desk and said, "I'm Elizabeth Kendrick here to register my family." They were shown two adjoining rooms; they had decided she and Lily would share and Freddy and Will the same.

Elizabeth was no sooner in her room when she was overcome with a great weariness. She stretched out on the bed, closed her eyes, and barely heard Lily close the door. Some while later, Lily returned, with Freddy trailing behind her. "I met another family travelling on the same ship, Momma," she said, eyes shining. "And there's a girl my age."

"Lovely. Did you see your father downstairs?"

"I wasn't going to tell you. He's sitting in the lounge talking to another man. Do you want me to get him?"

"No, let him be. There'll be few times left for that in England."

Two days later, they caught a ride to the dock, found their ship, got rid of the trunks, and were among the first to board. "Not as beautiful as the Titanic," Lily said.

"Hopefully, safer," said Elizabeth, tapping the railing.

The seas were calm for the first week of the voyage, then turned choppy. The dining room was deserted. When they reached the vicinity of the sinking, the captain held a Memorial Service and dropped a wreath overboard. Earlier, an announcement said anyone wishing to do the same, to contact the purser. Elizabeth was not surprised when Lily and her new friend flung a wreath into the churning waters.

On the evening before arriving in Halifax, the ship scheduled a gala event. Dress was semi formal. "I don't have anything suitable," said Elizabeth, glancing at her serviceable navy jumper. "Perhaps we should have a quiet dinner in our stateroom."

"No!" said Lily. "I'll find something to wear." She appeared later in a dark skirt, a long scarf wrapped around her slim waist, fastened with a brooch of brilliants. She had purchased a shawl in the ship's gift shop that nicely covered the scars on her neck. She looked stunning.

Elizabeth had managed to dress up a long skirt and pearl buttoned blouse with matching pearl necklace and earrings. Freddy decided his Sunday suit would do.

Will was the surprise of the evening. He had donned militia trousers and jacket worn with a white shirt and gold cufflinks. "You could be taken for a ship's officer," said Elizabeth, who'd had no idea he'd brought the clothes.

Lily went ahead of the family to find a table close to the band. Later in the evening she joined her new friend, and before long two young men joined the girls.

"Our Lily looks happy," said Will. "She'll make out all right in the new country."

The ship arrived in Halifax well before the family was awake. From the deck they saw workers scurrying about on the dock below unloading boxes and crates and various items. They ate a quick breakfast, gathered their belongings, and joined the crowd lining up to leave the ship.

Elizabeth checked her bag for the immigration papers, took Will's arm and followed everyone down the gangplank to the dock, where a sign directed them to the immigration office. She had the papers ready when she reached the front of the line. Everything was in order and before she knew it, they were back outside searching for their trunks.

The plan was to stay overnight in Halifax before catching the train to travel west to the town of Brandon, Manitoba, where a member of the family they were staying with would drive them to their nearby farm. In the meantime, they had to find their hotel for the night. Fortunately, immigration had reserved it close to the dock. After looking about the neighborhood of the hotel, and dinner, they retired to their rooms ready for an early start.

At the train station, the family found loading and unloading the trunks exhausting. They finally handed everything to a porter to put in the baggage compartment, found their seats and sat back. The family gazed at Elizabeth expectantly. She opened the folded table between them, and said, "This is what we're going to do from now on."

"After we leave the family on the farm, we're on our own, free to go where we want." She placed a newspaper on the table. "There's an ad here for hotels in the Kootenays that are looking for help, this one in Sirdar struck my fancy."

"How long are we staying with these people, Momma?" asked Lily. "Why are we going there?"

"It's an immigration requirement, that's all I know. Seems they want us to get used to Canadian ways. I expect the families get paid for having us. Anyway, we'll stay no more than three months. I want to be on the way to British Columbia before winter sets in. I gather Manitoba gets terribly cold."

Will shook his head and picked up the newspaper. "Have we become members of the gypsy tribe?"

She patted his hand. "It will all work out. Trust me."

He smiled. "I always do, Bessie."

She continued holding his hand. "Before we start working, I'd like to visit James and Gladys in Vancouver, stay a few days with them. From what I've read, it's a roundabout route to Creston. But I had the idea we could leave the trunks in Vancouver, have James ship them later."

Will looked up from the paper. "That's the best idea I've heard in a long time."

Elizabeth opened a bag that held sandwiches and passed them out. They spent their time looking at brochures, and out the window until a porter opened the berths for the night. The next day was the same.

When they reached Brandon, they were immediately approached by a sandy-haired man wearing overalls and a big smile. "I'm Lenny," he said as he loaded the trunks into the back of a farm cart. No one spoke until they'd driven through a gate and arrived at a farmhouse that included several outbuildings. Lenny pointed to one of the larger buildings. "That's been fixed up for you," he said.

Although the house they would live in was far from classy, Elizabeth decided they would make do. They tacked up a drape to provide privacy for Lily and Freddy's shared room and strung a line to hold their clothes. The kitchen stove looked impossible to cook on, and they did not require it for heat, so they arranged dinners with the family, agreeing to settle costs at the end of their stay.

Sadie, their host, was a chatty, cheerful woman who fussed about to make them comfortable. She showed Lily how to bake an apple cake and whip up pancakes. Lenny gave Freddy and Will fishing rods and pointed to a pond well stocked with fish.

Elizabeth used the time on the farm to rest, taking short walks near the house, and spending afternoons in a rocking chair. She accompanied Sadie and Lenny to church most Sundays and learned to use dollars instead of pounds at a village store.

Elizabeth and Lily watched for the frequent summer storms that suddenly brought frightening zigzag flashes of lightning and thunder and heavy rain never seen in England. When this happened, they took refuge in the pantry.

Will, fascinated by the storms, watched from a chair on the porch. Before they knew it, summer was over, and it was time to say goodbye. Lenny hitched the cart to the horses, loaded their baggage and drove them into Brandon to catch the train west to Vancouver.

James was a middle son of the Dane family, away at school when Elizabeth was born. She remembered him as a quiet young man who sometimes teased her. His older brothers arranged his gardening apprenticeship a day's drive from home, so he was rarely at the hotel. After he married Gladys, and emigrated to Canada, he lived in Nelson, a city in British Columbia. When his wife was unhappy, feeling enclosed by the mountains, the couple moved to the coast. Unfortunately, James could not find employment as a gardener in Vancouver and was obliged to take a job delivering gardening supplies.

By being careful, they had saved enough money to buy a Model T and were immensely proud of it. James pointed out its features as he loaded in the family's trunks and drove to the bungalow they were renting in the west end. The house was small, but it did have two bedrooms, one shown to Elizabeth and Will for their stay. The children would sleep in a basement room.

Elizabeth had met Gladys only once but had heard she could be critical. This was apparent when shortly after their arrival, she invited Lily into the bedroom to give her a gift. When Lily left the bedroom, carrying a basket of creams and bottles of oil, she appeared upset. She rushed past her mother and disappeared downstairs. Elizabeth took her by the arm when she reappeared with dried streaks on her face. "What's happened?"

The tears started up again. "Auntie gave me something to put on my face. She said it might improve my appearance."

Elizabeth found Gladys in the kitchen starting supper. "You've made our Lily cry with your foolish suggestions. What's wrong with you?"

"Is she so sensitive?"

"Only when she's with the likes of you!" Elizabeth swept out of the room.

Their words caused a cooling between them. Noting this James suggested an outing. The next day they left the car at the ferry terminal and crossed Burrard Inlet to catch a streetcar to Lynn Valley, a new community. When they arrived home, feelings between Elizabeth and Gladys had smoothed out.

When the visit was over, James agreed to store the trunks and ship them later. He drove the family to the train, shook hands with Will, kissed Elizabeth, and Lily, and slipped a two-dollar bill into Freddy's hand.

After a trip that involved changing trains, the weary family stepped down on the platform in the Village of Creston. They had saved money by going without a berth, and since there were few passengers, had stretched out on double seats, purchasing sandwiches from a vendor.

Elizabeth motioned the family to a bench outside the station. She was worried about William, who looked worn out from the train's sleeping arrangements. He'd regained his health from the stroke and earlier heart attack, although he'd dropped twenty pounds from rugby playing days. It was more a change in personality. No doubt the loss of the business and money worries and travel to another country were taking its toll.

Noting all of this, afraid he might collapse, she said, "Lily, come with me inside to ask about a hotel for the night." They were given the name of a hotel within walking distance, and lugging their smaller bags trudged along a rough road they'd never find in England.

The following morning, leaving Will and Freddy still in the room asleep, Elizabeth and Lily boarded a horse-drawn cart for the one-hour trip to Sirdar, a community of a few hundred people to check out the advertised hotel positions.

The Lookout Hotel was situated at the far end of the town's main street next to the horse terminal with a For Sale sign posted on the gate. Other than its spectacular view of the lake, the hotel was unimpressive. Next to it was a general store, and a few paces along, Jimmy's Eating House.

"We'll forget this place," said Elizabeth and she turned back toward Jimmy's. Over a bowl of soup, by asking a few questions, they heard the Lookout was barely hanging on, and they were given directions to the Garden Inn.

Elaine Granger, the contact mentioned in the ad, was sitting at her desk, the office door open. After introductions, she explained she needed someone to supervise the dining room and staff while she and her husband took a vacation. She gave Elizabeth's references only a fleeting glance.

Occasionally, as it happens when meeting a new person, one has the feeling they've known them for years. That's the way it was with Elaine and Elizabeth as they chatted about responsibilities of the six-month position that came with small suite.

Well satisfied with this news, Elizabeth and Lily caught the horse-cart back to the hotel in Creston. The Garden Inn was quiet weekdays, giving Lily a chance to learn the routine for waiting table under a head girl. But, on Sundays, Elizabeth gave a hand. The dining room was closed to the public on Mondays with meals served only to hotel guests. The family took advantage of this free time.

The days moved ahead. Freddy celebrated his fifteenth birthday in October. He kept busy with small chores about the hotel and found work at the general store unpacking boxes. Elizabeth was unsure how Will put in his time. He rose late after she left the suite for her office which was situated close to the dining room. When she returned to the suite he was sitting out back in an enclosed porch. She wondered how he spent his time from one until five until one afternoon returning from the post office, she saw him a half block away hurrying toward the hotel, a small sack under his arm.

When the holiday season arrived in December, Elizabeth hired three local girls to handle the numerous parties and dinners. Lily was kept busy and had little time for the family. To make the day festive, Elizabeth set a table in the suite for their Christmas dinner prepared in the hotel kitchen. The policy of the hotel was to close after Boxing Day, then reopen for a gala New Year's Ball, an event solidly booked mainly by people from Creston.

Then, everything became quiet, and the extra staff was let go. When a snowstorm closed the road between Creston in January, Elizabeth used the time to discuss the family's future with Will.

"As you know my contract ends in two months. We need to live in a larger community where Lily and I can find permanent employment. We're sure to find this in Nelson. I'd like to save a little more money to buy a small property. You'd like to get established, Will?"

"Gladys didn't have anything good to say about Nelson," said Will.

"I doubt she'd say anything good about any place," said Elizabeth.

"When we've saved enough, we'll look for a small property outside the city—space to have goats, definitely chickens. You'd like a dog, Will?"

He smiled. "That I would, Bessie. Doubt I can find a hound, though."

"I've always been partial to spaniels." Said Elizabeth. "So that's settled."

About the same time that Lily celebrated her seventeenth birthday, the Grangers wrote to say they'd be home in the first week of April. The political climate in Europe was a worry with talk of war. When they arrived home, the two families dined together and said farewell like ships passing in the night. Elaine handed Elizabeth a thank you card that included a bonus check for fifty dollars. The following morning, the family left to stay overnight at the same hotel in Creston before catching the train west.

Although Nelson was not far from Creston, it was a difficult place to reach. When they finally arrived on a beautiful spring day, Elizabeth said she would never leave. They checked their bags at the railway station before walking along Baker Street. Finding a place to stay was first on the agenda.

When they found a rooming house on a side street, Elizabeth said, "Come inside with me, Lily, we'll see what they offer." She stared up at the narrow three-story building that appeared to once have been a hotel. This was confirmed by a manager who said the rooms had been converted into suites. After listening to what they needed, she gave Elizabeth a key, suggesting they look around.

As they walked from one room to another on the second and third floors, Lily was unusually quiet. Suddenly she said, "Momma, I need my own room, I can't keep sharing with Freddy. I expect he feels the same way."

Elizabeth was about to say that it was only for a short while when the expression on Lily's face made her pause. "Let's go back downstairs and talk to the woman," she said instead. They ended up taking three rooms and one month turned into three.

Immediately, Lily and Elizabeth started looking for work, reading the ads in the daily paper and checking the various notice boards about town. There was no shortage of work, everything from waiters, dishwashers, even a cook. Lily found work before her mother, waiting table, starting early serving the breakfast crowd. Because she had taken a room at the end of the hall, and was away early in the morning, she only saw the family at dinner, which they ate at a restaurant next door to the rooming house.

Elizabeth had tried to create a cozy sitting area in their room by shifting the furniture about, but it was far from ideal. She was sitting across from Will following dinner one evening, when he said, "You're awfully quiet, Bessie, are you worried about us?"

She was surprised at his question. Up until now he'd given no opinion on most anything. "I'm a little disappointed that I haven't found work yet. I expect something will turn up. I've been thinking about our Lily. She's grown up a lot since we left home, maybe it was happening before. I've come to depend on her more than I should. I must cut the apron strings, let her be her own person."

"She'll do that without our help," said Will.

Lily's hours changed to a split shift starting at ten, ending at eight p.m. with two free hours in the afternoon. She often joined her mother for afternoon tea. Following her break, one afternoon, she handed Elizabeth her room key. "Do you mind taking my laundry bag when you do yours, Momma?"

"Not at all. I'm going over to the Heritage Hotel on Baker Street. They've advertised for an experienced person for the dining room."

Elizabeth had not been in Lily's room for over a week, there being no need. It was neat in the way Lily was, toilette articles laid out in a row on an enamel tray. She picked up a small jar of cream and screwed the top on tighter and set it back beside a tiny bottle of oil. From all appearances, Lily was experimenting with makeup. The next day she made a point of looking at Lily's complexion. In a subtle manner, Lily had blended the cream with the oil and applied it to the lower part of her face.

Elizabeth was successful in getting the dining room position that involved six hours, three days a week, starting at ten, ending at four in the afternoon. The hours meant she could join Will for a sherry before going out for dinner. Although their rooms were working reasonably well, the space was limited. The time had come to find a permanent home.

Lily had become dissatisfied with her job, and she had found another position at the Empress Hotel on Baker Street that provided room and board. Freddy had found work at a hardware store and was learning the business of clerking. This made Elizabeth realize the children were going their own way.

Elizabeth and Will were alone in the room. The days had become cooler. Will was wearing worsted trousers and a bulky sweater. His face was peaked. He'd pulled his chair close to the radiator.

She moved to sit beside him. "My dear, I'm going to ask Lily on her day off to come with me to find a realtor. With what we brought with us and what I've saved, we've enough to buy a small property out of town." She took his hand. "Time to make a proper home for you, enough of these rooms. And get you a dog."

A small smile lit his face. "I'd like that, Bessie. There's a number of kennels about."

Arm in arm, Elizabeth and Lily walked along Baker Street looking for a realtor's office, finally spotting one. He introduced himself as Harry Parker. Elizabeth quickly told him what they were looking for: two bedrooms, a good-sized kitchen with eating space—a dining room or is that too much to expect? A parlor, of course.

"Best if it's all on one floor—I have an ailing husband and I'm not getting any younger."

Harry Parker looked at his recent listings. "Not an awful lot in your price range, Mrs. Kendrick, especially when you want a bit of land. Give me a minute to check the old listings." He pulled a sheet of paper from a stack. "This has been on the market for a while. Needs a bit of work. If your son is going to live with you, he can spruce the place up."

"*A two-bedroom house on a quarter acre, large garden needs tender loving care. Shed for animals.*"

"The couple who lived there kept goats," the realtor added. "You thinking of getting animals?"

"A dog, maybe two dogs, chickens for sure, that's about it. Where is this place?"

"That's the thing. It's up the hill from the ferry slip across the lake at a place called Taghum. I could drive you there to look," he checked his watch. "Been empty since last fall. If you're free we could now."

Harry Parker was one of few who owned a car, its canvas window blinds rolled up to ventilate. He kept up a running conversation while driving to the ferry and while they waited for it to arrive. "The community has its own school, a post office and general store," he pointed out. "Fishing's good. Far as I see it, the one obstacle to owning the place is how to get back and forth into Nelson."

As they drove up the hill, Lily said, "It's a pretty place, Momma, but how would you get to work?" This was not a problem for Lily because her new job gave room and board.

It did not take long to view the property. The house surrounded by a vast overgrown garden, needed painting. Inside, both bedrooms were small, but the kitchen was roomy with an adjoining pantry. The parlor papered in red roses was a reasonable size, but the windows were small, although one gave a view of the lake. Fleetingly, Elizabeth recalled the elegant townhouse they'd left behind in England, and she exchanged a small smile with Lily who knew exactly what her mother was thinking.

Two straight-backed chairs had been left in the kitchen. Elizabeth sat down and faced the realtor. "It has possibilities. The main problem is transportation to Nelson. It needs thinking about. I don't see any great lineup to buy the place. After we talk it over, I'll get back to you."

They drove down the hill to the ferry slip, Elizabeth trying to visualize living here. She touched the realtor's arm. "If it's not too much trouble, could we stop at the store?" He nodded and parked outside a large square building. "I'll only be a minute," she said.

Inside she found what she was looking for, a message board beside the door. She ripped a page from her notebook, and wrote her name and where she was staying, and that she required a return ride into Nelson three days a week. She tacked it to the board.

A quick look outside showed no sign of the ferry, giving her time to buy a bunch of bananas and bag of candy. Back in Nelson, the realtor dropped them off at the rooming house.

Lily followed her mother to her room where Will sat by the window, a blanket over his shoulder. Elizabeth set the kettle on the hotplate and began to brew tea. "I can make something of the place if I can solve the transportation problem," she said. "But there is another matter to consider. Freddy would have to stay in town, come home weekends." They went back and forth on the subject, with little input from Will.

"We'll let it rest, see if I get an answer to my note," Elizabeth finally said.

A week went by, Lily started her new job at the Empress and moved her belongings there. The realtor called Elizabeth to ask if she had any more thoughts about buying the property, adding the owner was prepared to reduce the price. Freddy learned he could sleep in a small room at the back of the hardware store, act as night watchman. Elizabeth discussed the option of working three days in a row in the hotel dining room rather than daily. Everything fell nicely into place except she'd had no answers to her note.

Elizabeth was sitting in the room pondering what she could do when a cleaning girl rapped on the door to say a man was asking to see her. A farmer from Taghum who made daily runs to Nelson with vegetables in the growing season, and cut firewood in winter, had seen her note. He was agreeable to letting her ride with him, pick her up at the bottom of the Taghum hill. He'd work out a charge and let her know.

When Lily arrived home from work, in a worried voice, Elizabeth said "I don't want to agree to anything too binding."

"Go for it, Momma."

So, it was done, and now her savings account had a big hole in it. Harry Parker drove them to what she now called the ranch and left them at the door with several bags of groceries. Elizabeth's stomach took another downward turn.

Part 3

Lily worried that she was prevented from visiting her parents on the ranch while she learned her dining room duties at the Empress Hotel. She knew her mother had purchased a small amount of furniture at a second-hand store in Nelson, a bed and dresser, kitchen table and chairs, two easy chairs for the parlor, and a few odds and ends. They were to be delivered late in the day they moved in. She had also bought a box of kitchen dishes and cutlery at the local hardware store.

"Anything else we need, I can get from the store in Taghum," she assured Lily. "Freddy can use an old wagon I found in the shed to bring everything up the hill."

Lily's first day free from work was on a Wednesday. The head girl of the dining room said to confirm the time with Doris Smart, the hotel owner/manager, because the woman was known to change her mind.

On the day that Lily was hired, the woman promised Lily that she would have Sunday off as well. "Make sure you're back in good time to set the tables for breakfast," she reminded, unsmiling.

Preparing for her first day off, Lily had arranged a ride to the ferry, walked on but hadn't worked out her return trip.

She climbed the hill to the house and arrived in good time to find Freddy pulling weeds in the garden. He'd already raked the path to the house and got rid of refuse. She waved and rapped on the door and called out, "Momma?"

In the few days since she'd seen her mother, Lily saw the old house was shaping up. There was a round rug in the parlor with two chairs beside a wood stove. Against the far wall stood a tall desk with a few items that Lily recognized set on the shelf. "Very nice. Where did you get it?"

Elizabeth smiled. "It was being sold on consignment at the store. The man who owned it brought it from England. He's selling out."

"It really adds to the room," said Lily. "So, what can I do to help out? And where is Dad?" She had started to call her father Dad instead of Dada after she was teased when they lived in Sirdar.

"I asked him to make a start on the chicken pen. I have ordered six hens from the store. That store is amazing, Lily. They have everything, and what they don't have, they order in."

Lily stayed until four o'clock, then left to find a way back to Nelson. She was relieved that her mother had everything under control, and that her father was making himself useful. She said her goodbyes with a promise to meet for tea soon. The ferry was waiting at the dock for passengers, and she begged a ride with one of them into Nelson.

Her work at the hotel went reasonably well, other than getting along with Doris Smart, who did not warm to Lily. But the pay was good, and Lily tried to stay out of the woman's way. Lily did not get back to the ranch for several weeks, but sometimes she met her mother in Nelson for a quick cup of tea during each of their breaks. Elizabeth's enthusiasm about living at the ranch quietened Lily's fears.

Uncle James had followed through his promise to ship the trunks to the ranch where everyone was busy unpacking them.

Freddy finished classes at the local school and received a diploma. He agreed to stay the winter helping his parents rather than taking the hardware job in Nelson. He'd be sixteen in the fall and already had his eye on Ellen, a local girl, who lived with her parents on property near the ferry slip.

Will had settled into life on the small property. He bought a rooster to set among the hens, and at the same time brought home two mixed breed pups that he called Bonny and Brewster. In between chasing the rooster, they followed him around the property. Lily had never seen her father so content. Every other week he rode into Nelson with Elizabeth and Little Joe in the truck, finding his own way home. Elizabeth suspected he spent the day in the pub.

That winter they lost two hens to a fox getting into the pen but made up for the loss by a dozen chicks born in the spring. The remaining hens produced enough eggs to make up two baskets a week for Freddy to take down to the store. The clerk kept an account of the money earned and it was used for small purchases.

The Christmas mail from home arrived early, a parcel holding a plum pudding well wrapped in oil-skin, tied with linen string, several letters from various members of the family and one that held a bank note for 20 pounds from

George and Sophie. Elizabeth cashed the note and tucked the money away for emergencies.

Lily had four days off during Christmas and New Years and she spent it at the ranch sleeping in Freddy's room while he slept on the couch in the parlor. She helped her mother prepare roast goose for their dinner, and they boiled up the pudding for dessert. Will produced a bottle of brandy to toast in the new year. He drank more than he should and had to be helped to bed.

After the holiday, Lily rode into town with her mother and Little Joe. Back at the hotel, the holiday had not improved Doris Smart's mood.

After his first spurt of energy, Will slowed down, leaving the main chores to Freddy who worked at home and at the general store doing various jobs. Other than the treats he bought for Ellen who was now his steady girlfriend, he had no place to spend his money. He gave whatever he could to his mother to help.

With her egg money, and Freddy's contribution, along with her wages from the hotel and money that Lily gave her, the family was comfortably off. With the extra money Elizabeth bought a pine rocker for the kitchen and a set of shelves. She bought an upholstered stool and matching curtains for the bedroom.

Lily was popular with the dining room staff at the hotel. They laughed and teased her when someone at a table waiting to order called out, "Where's our Lily?"

Mother Elizabeth was also well liked at the hotel where she worked. She made several good friends, such as Edith, who often came for afternoon tea, while her children were at school.

Edith was several years older than Elizabeth. Her husband had enlisted and quickly was sent to England and then on to France right after he joined up in the 1914 war. She lived a few blocks from the hotel and Elizabeth usually served her tea, and if it was time for her own break, joined Edith. In this way Lily got to know Edith as well, and occasionally watched the children in the evening.

When Edith heard how Doris Smart was treating Lily, she said, "You'd best stay clear of that devil-woman. She's the jealous type, got rid of several girls when she thought they were making eyes at her husband."

"Really? I hardly ever see Mr. Smart."

"Doesn't matter. Watch yourself."

The year 1915 brought changes to the Kendrick family. Freddy, now seventeen, was itching to join the army. Most friends had departed for training or already were in England. He stayed home because of his parents and Ellen.

Edith's words of warning stayed with Lily. She carefully carried out her dining room duties and avoided contact with the manager. But she knew it was only a matter of time before they'd clash. It happened one afternoon when she was collecting a few items to take to the ranch the next day.

Doris called her in for a little chat. "I've decided to change your days off," she said. "Instead of Wednesday, I'm making it Thursday and Sunday will be only half day."

Lily had not expected Doris to hit hard where it mattered most. "But I've got a ride arranged and my mother's expecting me tomorrow," she said, her voice raising an octave. "And what good is a half day? The law says I'm to have two full days a week."

"Don't sass me, girl. If you do not like these arrangements, find another job."

"And that's exactly what I'll do," shot back Lily. "I'll finish my shift and pack up."

"I don't have to pay you—no notice or anything."

"You've been looking for a reason to discharge me from the first day," Lily said, and she slammed the door on the way out.

She returned to the dining room to set the tables for dinner. Pride made her leave everything in order. She dimmed the light, folded her apron, and set it on a chair and left for her room where she quickly packed her belongings in the suitcase kept under the bed. She stuffed the few items acquired for her mother into a shopping bag and left by the back stairs. When she got to the front door, Doris's husband, Eddy, was waiting for her.

He handed her an envelope. "Your pay," he said. "What do you plan to do now, young lady?"

Lily tossed her hair that had tumbled out of the bun. She was not about to admit she had no plans. "I've several ideas, and tonight I will stay with a friend, thank you."

"I'm sorry it came to this," he said, "my wife can be difficult."

Lily bit back her response and swept out. She hurried up Baker Street to Edith's house where she knew she would be welcome. She was bedraggled by the time she knocked on Edith's door and was swarmed by the children. Her suitcase had a deep scratch from being dragged. It did not take long to tell Edith why she was there.

"I knew this would happen," the woman said. "Tonight, you sleep on the couch and for as long as you need."

"I'll stay at the ranch with Momma and Dad until I figure what to do. Do you have a small bag I can transfer a few clothes in? I'll leave my big suitcase with you until I know what I'm doing."

"When I saw this, I thought of you," said Edith, handing Lily a page from the Nelson News.

After a quick look, Lily saw it was an ad for help needed at a hotel in Kaslo. "Where's Kaslo?"

"It's a pretty place on Kootenay Lake. The children and I went there once with George. Anyway, take the paper and look it over at home."

Lily reread the ad. "I'd have to think about leaving Momma." The next morning with a small bag she caught her ride to the ferry, and on the other side of the lake climbed the hill to the ranch. Her father was feeding the chickens when she arrived, the two dogs tagging along. She waved to him and entered the house, where her mother was busy setting the table for lunch.

As surprised as she was at hearing Lily had quit her job, Elizabeth did not have much to say, other than, "You'll find something." She always took a cheerful outlook.

Lily helped her mother finish setting the table, then pulled out a chair and sat down. "How are you and dad making out on your own?" Her brother had gotten his way and joined the army. He was somewhere on the prairie doing his training. She was careful not to mention the job in Kaslo.

"We're doing fine. I have a local boy helping with the chores. And I've another thought on my mind. I waited to talk to you before I decide."

"What's it about?"

"You know I'm in and out of the Taghum store, well, they asked if I wanted to work there. Seems the owner who does the books and buys supplies has joined up."

"What about your job at the hotel?"

"I'll let it go, Lily. I'm good with accounts and this would keep me close to home, better for your father. He gets lonely with me gone all day. And it means I won't have to ride back and forth with Little Joe."

Lily sat thinking. "How would you feel if I took a dining room job out of town? Dad is starting to slow down—can you manage on your own?"

Elizabeth hesitated, "I'd miss you stopping by, but you must make your own life," she smiled. "Freddy's girlfriend, Ellen, comes by almost every day, she misses Freddy dreadfully. I'll ask her to do a few extra things for me."

Lily's spirits lifted. "I'll still be sending money to help you out, Momma, and visit as often as I can. I make far more than I need," she took the hotel ad from her pocket and passed it to her mother. "Then, if you're okay, I'll write to find out more about this. I also think you should take the job at the store."

Lily wrote a short letter to the manager of the hotel in Kaslo with her qualifications and mailed it that evening. She settled in at the ranch taking over Freddy's room and helping her parents with various chores. She got to know Ellen and outlined what would be helpful to her mother, mainly, making lunch for her dad each day, and making a start on the dinner, for her mother had accepted the job at the store. Elizabeth, smartly dressed in an ankle length gray skirt and blouse with a wrap, left the house each morning shortly before ten and climbed the hill home before four.

Lily was into her second week at the house when she sat down with her father for a mid-morning coffee. She watched him stir sugar into his cup. "How do you like Canada, Dada," she said using the childish name. "Are you happy here on the ranch?"

He looked up, "I'm happy enough." He stood up and went to the cupboard over the sink and lifted down a bottle, poured a little into his coffee, returned the bottle to the cupboard and sat down.

Lily said nothing. She pushed a plate of cookies toward him and concentrated on making small talk until a rap on the door and Ellen entered. While they were chatting, she studied her father. Her mother had spared her from knowing much about his habits. She thought about her mother's frugal ways. Why had her father not found a job to help? Why did he continually sit in the house reading the paper or half asleep? He was only interested in the dogs. Why did her mother say nothing? This had to be love.

One afternoon when Lily had been at the house ten days, Elizabeth brought home a letter that had arrived at the store from the manager of the hotel in Kaslo. Frances Lang had been away visiting her daughter in Vancouver and just returned home. She suggested Lily find her way to Kaslo for an interview, and if mutually satisfied could start work immediately. Despite leaving her mother, Lily was excited about the offer, didn't even think it would not work out. She hugged her father, kissed her mother, caught a ride with Little Joe, retrieved her suitcase from Edith and after much effort arranged a ride to Kaslo. She arrived on a glorious spring day in 1916. She was nineteen years old.

Kaslo was a small lake community with a main street and several streets off it. Before going to the Lang Hotel for her interview Lily walked the four blocks down to the lake where the paddle-wheeler S. S. Moyie was docked. Then she carried on up the other side of the street noting two small hotels, one on a side street. What looked like a three story-building had multipurpose use, one being a museum. She had a cup of tea in a small café and carried on to the Lang.

Frances Lang, owner/manager, was behind the desk in the lobby when Lily arrived. "I've come about the dining room position, Ma'am," she said. "I received your letter that I should come with my qualifications."

"You got here in good time," Frances Lang said.

"Yes, I left as soon as I heard from you."

"We're somewhat out of the way. Did you have difficulty getting here?"

Lily smiled, "A bit. I took a few wrong turns, but eventually got it right."

"Good. We'll talk in the dining room. I expect you could do with a snack after travelling?"

"That would be nice," said Lily who was getting used to Canadian terms. After they were seated, she handed the woman the short list of places she had worked and length of time.

Frances Lang went into the kitchen and returned with a plate of sandwiches and a pot of tea. "This hotel is the main establishment in town," she began, "formerly called the Willows, but my husband, Edward Lang, changed the name to the Lang Hotel, plain and simple," she said as she poured the tea. "He's owned the hotel twenty-five years, well before I arrived as a young girl from Montana." A flicker of a smile crossed her face. "Much younger than you," she added.

She touched her face. "I don't want to appear rude but were you in an accident?"

Most adults avoided mentioning Lily's scars. Some just turned away. She hesitated, "I was five years old helping my mother bake little cakes on an open fire when a spark flew up onto my dress. The flames were everywhere."

"You poor child!"

"I'm used to how I look, Ma'am." Lily took one of the sandwiches.

"We all have things in our life we'd like to change," said Frances Lang. She picked up one of the sandwiches and ate it. "We have a regular clientele that have their meals here, people from the government office and the police station. We serve plain, wholesome food and open early for breakfast. How will all of this suit you?"

"I'm fine with how everything is arranged. Would I have a room in the hotel and my meals?"

"Of course. There are two rooms, a sitting area and bathroom on the top floor for staff. The eight rooms on the second floor are for salesmen who stay a night or two." She bit into another sandwich, passed the plate to Lily. "I can tell by your accent you're English. Did you come over with your family?"

"Yes, Ma'am, my mother and father and brother, whose serving in the war. I've been in Canada four years."

"Well, Lily, the job is yours if you want it. Do you need to think it over?"

"No, Ma'am. I'm pleased to take the job."

"I think you should call me Frances, we're quite casual here. My husband, though, likes to be addressed as Mr. Lang, he's twenty years older than me. I'm curious, Lily, where did you learn to wait table?"

Lily's face broke into a smile. "From my mother, Ma'am, there's nothing she doesn't know about hotel work, including waiting table. Her family owned and managed hotels for years and years. I can thank my mother for everything I know."

"Your mother sounds like a remarkable woman, I'd like to meet her," said Frances Lang.

Lily took the rest of the day settling into one of the rooms on the upper floor, and the next morning stood at the entrance to the dining room awaiting instructions for the day. She wore an ankle length navy skirt with white blouse and had tucked a polka dot blue and white scarf into the neck. When her first shift was over, she wrote home, "I got the job, Momma. I think I'll be happy here. The woman in charge is nothing like that other horrible person."

Frances Lang took a liking to Lily, and two months after starting the job, invited her to dinner at her home located two blocks from the hotel on the main street. Surrounded by lilacs in summer bloom, the house, built in the style of an English home, reminded Lily of her uncle George's place. It was quite lovely, she thought as stood on the upper step looking back at the street before she rang the bell.

Lily had met Edward Lang several times when he stopped by the hotel dining room for afternoon tea with his wife. He was pleasant in a formal way, which didn't bother her because she was used to her mother's brothers, especially Uncle George.

The earlier dinner invitation at the Lang house became one of several over the next year. In the last few months that Lily had worked at the hotel, and dinner guests often included Jack Williams, a young policeman stationed in Kaslo. Lily and Jack met in the dining room a short while after Lily started work there. She was standing in the entrance with a tray of coffee, Frances beside her. "Who is that good looking man sitting by the window?" Lily asked.

"Oh, that's our local policeman. Would you like to meet him?"

"I wouldn't mind," said Lily. "I'll bring him a fresh coffee." And that's how it began.

John (Jack) Williams spent all but one year of his life in the small community of New Denver, British Columbia. His parents divorced, and mother, Iris, remarried a BC Provincial Police Officer living in Nelson. When Jack was choosing a career, his stepfather suggested the police force was a good one to pursue.

After spending a year at his first post in the town of Fernie, Jack was transferred to Kaslo. He'd been there about six months when Lily was introduced to him in the dining room of the Lang Hotel. As a police officer, he was exempt from conscription, but seeing so many of his friends joining up, he planned to do the same.

There was an immediate attraction between Lily and Jack. Within days he'd asked her to join him for dinner. When hockey season arrived, she attended many of his games and on several occasions accompanied him on the train to the town of Sandon to watch him play. He had made a name for himself in the game. Lily told her parents about Jack, but they had not met him, and because his stepfather and mother had moved to Vancouver, she had not met them either.

In the summer of 1917, with the war still raging in Europe and no sign of it ending, the list of casualties grew longer and longer. Over one of their weekly dinners, Jack told Lily he was going to join up. "I can't stay here and let others fight for me," he said. He had a younger brother, Bert, now serving in France, where men were dying in droves in the trenches.

Lily and Jack had been seeing each other for a year, but there was no talk of marriage. She was only twenty, there was lots of time. But she also was aware of the casualties taking up pages in all the newspapers.

"I've been thinking what you said about your father, how his health is poor. Maybe if I join up you could go home for a visit, stay awhile," Jack suggested.

She teased him, "Are you afraid I'll meet someone else if I stay here?"

"I suppose you might. But no, that's not the reason I'm suggesting you go home. I know how much you miss your mother."

"I do. We're very close. Where do you enlist? Will you still be a policeman when you come home?"

He took her hand, "I'm glad you said 'when' and not 'if.'"

"Oh, Jack!" Her voice caught.

"I have to go to an office in Nelson. And according to what I'm told, my job will be waiting for me when I return, maybe not in Kaslo, but another detachment."

They were quiet for a moment. "If I wasn't going away, I'd talk to you about us having an understanding—now I'm not sure that's sensible."

"I don't imagine I'll find anyone I care for as much as you," she said. "I'd like an understanding—if that's what you want. In England when a couple spend time together it's called walking out."

"We've run, walked and hiked together. Is that the same thing? I'll understand if you change your mind while I'm gone. It'll be a month before I leave. That'll give you time to decide about everything."

Frances Lang was sorry that Lily was leaving. "Promise if you need a job you'll come back. I'll always find a place for you," she said, hugging Lily. "Don't forget us."

Lily accompanied Jack to the recruiting office in Nelson, waiting in a coffee shop while he filled out the papers. The way the war was going in Europe, he was sure the war department would be glad to have him. They sent him for a medical, and that's where a surprise waited for Jack. "You're very fit, but did you know that you have a goiter?" the doctor said.

"I don't even know what that is, let alone have it," said Jack.

"It's a condition that affects the throat. It will not change how you live, but it will exempt you from active duty on the front lines. You can still serve in other capacities. It likely will save your life. Some people would say you're lucky unless you get run over by a London double decker bus."

"You have a funny sense of humor," said Jack, shaking his head.

Jack slid onto the bench across from Lily at the restaurant. "Guess what?" He told her what the doctor had said. "So, looks like I'll live to be an old man." He chuckled at the thought.

"Do you ever see your real father?" she asked, suddenly.

"I make sure I don't," said Jack. "I gave up on him after he deserted me." He told her how as a fifteen-year-old he was scheduled to visit his father in Vancouver, and how the man had not turned up.

"What did you do?"

"I had only a little money, so I got hold of a bike and I delivered telegrams. One day I got sick, fell off the bike and the next thing I remembered I was in the hospital with rheumatic fever, or maybe it was diphtheria. They found my New Denver address with my bag. My sister lived somewhere in the area, she came to collect me, then I went home."

"I'm sorry, Jack. Oh, well, it worked out for you to meet me. Where is your sister now?"

He chuckled, "That's another story."

When they'd arrived in Nelson, they stopped by Edith's house where Lily introduced Jack and arranged to stay a few nights until he shipped out. He planned to say goodbye to his mother and stepfather on a stopover in Vancouver. Even before he caught the train, she felt lost. "You'll write as soon as you know where you're posted?"

"Of course." He got his instructions from the recruiting office, was given a slip to pick up his gear and his train schedule that included a stopover in Vancouver. From there he'd travel to a town in Quebec before shipping out. He'd be on the troop ship for two weeks, embarking at Plymouth before going to the Salisbury Plains for four months training. They'd tell him where to go from there.

"I hope they don't get mixed up and send you to France. Are you scared?" Lily asked, as they walked to the train, arm in arm.

"Of course not, maybe a bit excited. I've hardly been anywhere, not like you crossing the ocean, and moving all over the place."

She stopped and swung round to look at him. "You want to do this, don't you? It's all an adventure for you."

"I suppose—but I'll miss you, Lily."

The station was quiet as they waited for the train. They were quiet, too. Lily, who rarely cried, held back the tears. Then suddenly everything felt rushed with the train behind schedule and porters hurrying the passengers to get on.

"Go on," she said. "Don't get run over by a bus." She laughed through her tears.

She watched him mount the steps and disappear, reappear at a window in the second coach. "Never gets easy saying goodbye," said a woman standing beside her.

Lily was in a subdued mood when she arrived at Edith's house for her last night. As they sat over a late cup of coffee, Edith said, "You're upset because he was enthusiastic to get going, forgetting he was leaving you behind. That's the way with men, Lily. You must get used to it. After he's been away awhile, he'll wish he was home. I remember the first time my George left. He could hardly wait to get out the door. They sent him to some place in the east. He had a week's leave before going overseas and was dragging his feet when he left." She finished her coffee and sat back. "At least you know Jack will be somewhere safe, not getting shot up. While he's away you must make your own life, don't go mooning around feeling sorry for yourself."

Edith's words perked Lily up. In the morning she called Little Joe for a ride to the ranch, and by late afternoon was walking up the path to the ranch house. In the distance Ellen was carrying a pail to scatter grain for the chickens. Lily banged on the door and opened it. "I'm home, Momma."

Elizabeth was quite overwhelmed at the sudden appearance of Lily. She wiped her hands on the cloth she was using to dry dishes. "Why didn't you tell me you were coming? I hope you're not sick?"

"Course not, Momma. I forgot you don't like surprises. You look well—and dad?"

"Not much difference, no energy to speak of. He's out back sitting in an old chair. But tell me, why are you here so sudden?"

Lily told her about Jack joining the army, and what the recruiting officer had said. "He'll stay in England, won't be going to France, that's one good thing. Because he's an experienced police officer, his training won't be as long as some."

Elizabeth ushered her toward the door. "Go and find your dad while I put the kettle on for tea and give Ellen a call to join us. She's over the moon because our Freddy is coming home for good."

Lily paused at the back door. "For good?"

"Yes, he applied for a dispensation to help his aging parents, and it was granted."

"That's wonderful news, Momma. It'll be like old times for you and dad."

Not knowing when Freddy would arrive, Lily settled into his room for her stay. While there, they received a telegram he had docked in Halifax and would be home in ten days.

"I must start to think about my future, Momma," Lily said one morning over breakfast. She had spent her time at the house helping with the cleaning and the garden and getting to know Ellen who was likely to become a part of the family. "I've been looking at ads in the Nelson News. One looks interesting." She pushed the paper over to her mother to read.

"Wanted by CPR, Young Women to Replace Men Serving Overseas. Dining room work on Kootenay Lake Ships. Relevant Duties."

"Now that I don't need to worry about you and dad, I'm going to check this out. I'll ride into Nelson with Joe tomorrow."

"It appears you're what the CPR is looking for," said Elizabeth. "I know you're restless to find something."

"It's been lovely staying with you and dad, but it might be a long time before Jack comes home, and even then, circumstances may have changed between us." She laughed, "Besides, I must vacate Freddy's room."

Lily arrived at the CPR Personnel Office immediately after they opened for the afternoon. She gave a brief account of her dining room experience to the clerk, who said, "You're the first to answer our ad." He looked at her references. "I know the Lang Hotel in Kaslo. If you worked there that's a good enough reference. Why did you leave?"

"When my boyfriend, a police officer in Kaslo enlisted, I decided to go home. My parents live on a small ranch at

Taghum. My father is not well, and I thought I could help my mother."

He nodded and offered her cup of coffee from a pot warming on a hotplate. "We're looking for young women with your experience. Could you find us a few more like you?"

"I'm not sure but I could try."

He refilled her coffee cup, and said, "We need two or three girls to replace the boys who have left for overseas. We're short of staff." He explained that except for occasional relief work on the S.S. Moyie and the Kuskanook, their time would be spent on the Nasookin, the largest stern paddle wheeler to sail in BC waters.

"It was built in 1913, you can see it's quite new," he said proudly. "It carries 550 passengers and is luxurious and spacious. She leaves from Kaslo and travels down Kootenay Lake to Nelson, making various stops completing the run at Kootenay Landing before returning. The staff have two days off every week, either in Kaslo or Nelson."

"You have my permission to hire three girls, young lady."

"Thank you," said Lily. "I'll do my best." After leaving the office she went to the Nelson News on Baker Street where she placed an ad, followed by one for the Vancouver Sun. Two experienced girls from Vancouver answered, and a girl who'd worked with Lily in Kaslo replied from Nelson. Lily decided to hire her despite the girl being a little slow. Within a month, all four were settled on the Nasookin for its daily five-hour run.

Before starting work Lily stayed on at the ranch sleeping on the couch because Freddy had come home. She was glad she was still there because she received her first letter from Jack. He had survived the voyage despite being seasick most of the first week. The letter was written from the coastal town of Eastbourne where he was serving as a guard for a hospital that originally was home for the Davis family. "The lady of the house reminded me of you, very elegant, with perfect manners," he wrote, causing Lily to smile.

Now that she knew Jack was safely located, Lily was content. She sorted out her belongings to take onto the ship where she would have a good-sized stateroom. She said goodbye to the few friends she'd made in Taghum. Ellen and Freddy got engaged during the time Lily was at the ranch. He'd bought her a single diamond ring from his army pay. They said the wedding was still a long time away.

Lily spent a night with Edith before leaving. The distance between Nelson and Kaslo was not huge, but the route was difficult. Little Joe said he had to take her the long way because the ferry that crossed the lake had broken down and was in repairs for at least a week. He'd drive her as far as New Denver where she had to find her own way to Kaslo.

They were travelling along the river through farm communities, when Little Joe said "We're about to approach two tunnels, nothing to be nervous about. There's talk about moving the road higher up but that would cost scads of money. I doubt it'll be in my lifetime." She spent the next three hours gazing at the marvelous scenery.

When they reached New Denver, he drove straight to the New Market Hotel situated at the foot of the main street. If she recalled the story, Jack had told her, this was where his mother had stayed when first arriving from Manitoba with her two children.

Little Joe had a meal in the hotel with Lily before starting back home. While there he found out there was a twice weekly truck that dropped men at the mines between New Denver and Kaslo. Unfortunately, she'd have to wait until the end of the week for the next run. He suggested she put her name down on the passenger list.

After being given a comfortable room on the second floor of the hotel, and looking around the neighborhood, Lily retired for the night. The next day she explored the town that Jack grew up in. Although, none of his family lived there now, the name was well known. She found the family home, and the building that housed his mother's dry goods and dressmaking business. It stood empty.

She walked through the lakeside park where a forlorn grandstand stood. Jack had told her about the May Day celebrations here, and how on the 24th all the children removed their shoes—unless the weather was perfectly horrible—and didn't put them on again until September. She was glad she'd had to stay in New Denver for those few days, it brought Jack closer to her.

When Lily arrived in Kaslo on the Friday she went to the Lang Hotel for a room. She was not scheduled to report to the Nasookin until the Monday. Edith Lang was shocked to see Lily and insisted she come for dinner to tell her about the new job. "That's wonderful, much more exciting than working at the Lang." They spent the weekend catching up on the news.

It didn't take Lily long to settle into her new work on the ship, and soon it was if she'd been there forever. Her experience in dining rooms served her well. Before long she became the Head Girl, serving only the captain's table while supervising the staff.

Handling Rosa, one of the Vancouver girls, was another matter. The pretty brunette in her frilly apron turned the eye of every travelling salesman she looked at, and there were many on the lake run. Lily overlooked her behavior for the first month until she saw Rosa slipping out of a stateroom. She confronted Rosa. "I spotted trouble from your first day and regret hiring you. You're man crazy, fooling around every chance you get."

Rosa responded by going for Lily's hair, yanking it loose from the neat bun.

"You're jealous," she shouted. "Because no one looks at you with scars on your face."

Lily responded with a shove that pushed Rosa against the stateroom door. The captain on his way for afternoon tea heard the ruckus. He stepped into the stateroom and grabbed Rosa by the arm and hauled her down the passageway. In the skirmish Lily received a deep scratch on her face. The captain ordered Rosa to stay in her stateroom. "It's off the ship with you the next stop," he said.

Two miles up the lake at a small settlement, not a regular stop, the Nasookin nosed into shore and the crew tossed out the gangplank. Normally, a community would alert the ship to stop by tying a white rag to a stick. Rosa stumbled off the ship and disappeared down the road to find her own way home. Not long after this, one of the older girls quit, replaced by a summer student.

"I'm glad to see the back of the lot," said Roger, the purser. He wasn't smiling as usual, and it was several months before Lily knew why.

She was walking along Baker Street in Nelson on her two days off spent with her parents at the ranch when she saw a shabby man wearing an old raincoat and flapping sandals leaning against the bank building. She had wondered why Roger had suddenly disappeared from the ship, had assumed he found a better job. Now here he was, holding out his hand, the neatly dressed man she remembered gone.

"Whatever in the world has happened to you?" she said, taking his arm.

He told her his story. "I've no one else to blame but myself. They accused me of grafting, pocketing money from passengers buying their tickets. A spotter turned me in. I can't get a job anywhere. I've even had to sell my clothes."

Lily felt sick at the news. She considered Roger a good friend, had shared many cups of tea with him on their breaks. "You're a wreck," she said. "Oh, my…your clothes, your shoes…she was at a loss for words."

"I wondered for old times if you could spare me a bit of change," he said.

"I don't know what to think, I'm so upset." She handed him two dollar bills, and stepped back, shaking her head. Roger's plight stayed with Lily for the rest of the afternoon. Instead of browsing the stores she returned to Edith's house where she was staying.

In March 1917, Lily turned twenty-one, the day celebrated with the crew aboard the ship. The weekend before she had a family celebration on the ranch. Although her mother said she was well, she appeared more tired. Her father rallied to join her birthday party. To her youthful eyes he appeared increasingly frail. Freddy had gained back the weight he lost while serving in the army. She suspected he indulged too much in Ellen's cooking.

Since joining the ship when it overnighted in Nelson, Lily got into the routine of visiting the family, making time to see Edith and look around the stores. Generally, spirits were low because the war, into its third year, dragged on. Regular as clockwork, Jack wrote, sometimes only a postcard. She was often asked out by the young men who she worked with, and at first had declined, but after the months turned to a year then two, she accepted the dinner dates always explaining that she had a steady boyfriend overseas.

Early in 1918, she was promoted to Matron, responsible for women who came aboard the ship, many with children. She still waited on the captain's table, and often at the end of the meal when the passengers had left, joined him for a cup of coffee. She had opened a bank account in Nelson and had a tidy sum of money saved even after helping her parents. It was in the summer of that year that she realized she hadn't had her usual letter from Jack. She was not concerned until what had only been a few weeks turned into months. Pride kept her from telling the family or Edith. She knew nothing had happened to him because he'd left her address with his mother, and if he'd been in an accident, she'd have heard. Two years was a long time for them to be apart. She read over his last two letters where he mentioned going to London on leave. Had he met a girl there and took the easy way out by not writing?

To boost her spirits, Lily went shopping. She loved clothes and hats and bought only the best. She was strolling along Baker Street when she noticed a jewelry store that she often frequented was advertising welcome home gifts for servicemen. This was an optimistic touch on the part of the jeweler, she thought as she entered the shop.

"Hello, Miss Lily," the jeweler said. "Never overdressed, always beautifully dressed. What can I show you today?"

Cheered by his flattery, she said, "The cigarette case in the window."

"For your young man, I presume. When is he coming home?"

The war had turned for the better, and a trickle of married men, many with children were arriving home. She hesitated, unwilling to tell the man she had not heard from Jack for some time. "I expect he'll show up any day," she said cheerily. She paid for the case and left the store. Back on the ship she placed the tissue-wrapped case in the stateroom drawer.

With her new responsibilities Lily handed out extra soap and towels to families on their way to the coast to meet their husbands. Many of the children were in a filthy condition from travelling from all parts of the Kootenays. To assist a mother loaded with baggage, Lily often had to carry an infant off the ship to the waiting train in Nelson. Along with the women, came men looking for their old jobs back. She had received a letter saying her own position was secure.

The ship was docked in Nelson ending a three-day layover. On November 11, 1918, the war was officially over. Lily stood at the railing watching the crowds below with no desire to join them. Many carried flags or were tooting noisemakers. The boats at the wharf were adding to the celebration. One of the crew handed her a glass of champagne. "Cheers!" he said, and he kissed her soundly before sprinting away.

Six weeks later, after a visit with the family, where she'd enjoyed a Christmas dinner and heard Freddy and Ellen's wedding plans, Lily was standing at the elaborate dining room sideboard inspecting the tables for their evening meal. The room was attractively decorated with silver bells and garlands of holly, and lighted with three chandeliers that cast a pale glow on everything.

She had resigned herself to Jack's disappearance and accepted an invitation for the evening with a handsome young university student. With one last glance at the room and her mind on what she was going to wear for her date, she didn't notice a serviceman standing at the entrance talking to a waiter until he turned. Jack had boarded the ship without her knowing. All she could do was stare.

They were seated at a table when he said, "Didn't you know me?"

She took a deep breath. "I was shocked."

"I gather you're starting your days off," he said carefully. "We could have a late dinner?"

"I've already made dinner plans," she shot back. "Did you think I'd sit around waiting for you, no letters for months?"

"I guess not…you know I'm not much of a letter writer. I thought it more important that I came."

She picked up a starched napkin, folded and unfolded it. "I suppose under the circumstances I could break my dinner engagement. But, Jack, get this straight. You must be more considerate. Matters have to be right with us."

During World War 1, Lily is employed on the SS Nasookin (on Kootenay Lake) in dining room and later as Matron to replace men serving overseas.

Jack takes time out from policing in Clayoquot to go duck hunting. 1920

Studio portrait of Lily taken in Nelson about 1918, mailed to Jack who is overseas in World War I.

Lily strolls the beach with her beloved dogs, Lucky and Juno, in Kitimat, B.C. Following retirement from the B.C. Police, Jack is employed as Head of Security for Kitimat Construction.

Williams Family photo taken about 1939 in Vancouver shows Betty, Lily, June, Jack.

Part 4

With only an occasional change of names, the following section of *Lily's Journey* is a factual account of the lives of Lily and Jack from 1920 to 1943. The material was recorded by daughter Elizabeth through taped interviews along with other documents.

For the first few days Lily and Jack were shy with each other. They were apart for over two years, having different experiences, meeting different people. The time apart had changed them.

They had changed in other ways too. Lily had added five pounds to her petite form, which emphasized her curves. Jack had lost twice that and now was as lean as a greyhound. Still in uniform, wearing high polished boots instead of the wrap-around puttee that he thoroughly despised, he looked incredibly handsome.

After the first evening when Lily spoke her mind, she was more careful with her choice of words. She sensed that Jack felt the same strangeness between them. She wondered if anything would change this.

Lily took a week's holidays after Jack arrived in Nelson, staying with Edith and the children. George had been detained in London, but was expected to arrive home soon. Jack spent the week taking Lily to the theatre and various places, and finally got to meet her parents. It would be a short visit because Jack had to report to the government office in Kaslo to see if he had a job, as promised.

Lily had sent a message to her mother who waved from the door and ushered them into the parlor where she'd set a table with her best dishes for lunch. Her father was congenial throughout the meal asking Jack about his experiences in England. Freddy and Ellen, who'd joined them, helped carry the conversation. All in all, the time spent was very pleasant. "I'll be back to see you soon, Momma," Lily called from the door as they were leaving. "I'm staying on the ship for a while."

When they returned to Nelson, over dinner, Jack said, "Your mother is very gracious in the same way that Mrs. Davis—Olivia—is. A real lady."

"The English woman didn't mind you calling her by her first name?"

"Oh, for the first year I was very formal, then when other guards were transferred, and I was the only one, it was natural to call her by her first name. Before she married, she came from a titled family. I had many a meal at her small apartment. She adapted well after the army requisitioned her home for a hospital."

"There obviously was a Mr. Davis?"

"Oh, yes, twenty years older."

"I see," said Lily. "Sounds like she made your stay quite pleasant."

"Very," he said. "I told her all about you, Lily, and she's going to write to us."

The next day when Jack escorted Lily back to the ship, she said, "You'll let me know as soon as you hear about a job?"

Of course. If I'm lucky, it'll still be in Kaslo.

A week later Lily received a wire from Jack that an urgent family matter was sending him to Vancouver. She presumed his mother was ill, but it wasn't his mother, it was his younger brother, Bert.

Jack and Bert were fourteen months apart and were as close as two peas in pod. They even looked alike. As youngsters, they hiked the hills around New Denver, swam side by side to the far shore, two small fish in a pond. If one had a scab on his arm or a bruised knee, you could be sure the other would have the same. They even sounded alike which fooled their mother.

Bert enlisted in the army a year before Jack, and immediately was sent to France. Other than a shrapnel wound, he survived the war without a scratch. He was not so lucky when he was waiting to return home. Living in close contact with many others in the barracks, he contracted the Spanish Flu.

He wasn't too sick at first, managed to make it home to Vancouver, where along with his family, he had a girlfriend. They partied night and day, drank too much, lived it up. One morning, the girlfriend found Bert collapsed on the kitchen floor. He was rushed to Shaughnessy Hospital. That's where Jack visited him.

"You survived the war better than most, and just look at you," he said, taking his brother's hand through the protective screen.

"What got into you to behave in such a way?" Jack had heard about Bert's escapades.

Bert was past responding. He died two days later, his mother beside his bed.

Jack was devastated by his brother's death at age twenty-three. Nothing in his life so far had affected him this way. He bought a bottle of whiskey and returned to the hotel where he was staying, drinking into the night. He stayed in bed the next morning sick from the alcohol. He remained in Vancouver for the funeral, then wired Lily that he was coming home. "Would you please meet me in Nelson?" he asked.

He arrived at the hotel where Lily was staying; she was no longer staying with Edith because George had come home. "You look terrible. Tell me what this is all about?"

Slowly, she got the story from him. She had never met Bert, but it was as if she'd known him. Jack had a small snap of his brother taken by a buddy beside a tank in France. She could have been looking at Jack, they were so alike. She passed the photo back to him, wiped a rush of tears, and held out her arms to him. It had taken a tragedy to bring them close again.

When he was composed, he said his superintendent was looking for a place that needed police protection. All he'd found, so far, was one that hadn't been occupied for years. "Do we still have an understanding?" he asked, shyly.

"I suppose."

"Good. Then when I hear something more, I'll tell you. I suppose we should get married?"

She wiped away the last of the tears. "That's probably a good idea—we don't want to be living in sin."

Jack returned to Kaslo. He found the only available post that was livable was at Clayoquot on Stubbs Island on the BC coast. Before agreeing, his chief suggested Jack inspect the site to see if it was satisfactory. Lily and Jack postponed their June marriage to the fall to give him time to check out the site.

When he returned, he boarded the SS Nasookin to talk to Lily. "I've had a look, and the place is in terrible condition. The roof leaks, the stove is rusted out, there was a foot of sand on the floor from an open window. The place hasn't been occupied for years, well before the war. I did what I could to clean it up and patched the roof, but I don't think I can take you there, Lily. It's not fit for an animal, let alone my bride."

She looked thoughtful. "You say there's nothing else available if you wait?"

"According to the Chief, there isn't. I could try to find another line of work."

"They might not take you back if you leave. Can the place be made livable?"

"With a lot of work, I suppose it could. Someone has trucked in soil to make a garden at the back, all overgrown now. The house is a good enough size. Needs white washing and painting."

"Then I think you should take it," she said. "When Momma moved to the ranch it was also in a bad state. You've seen what she made of it."

Lily decided to leave the ship in Nelson. The time was right, for the vessel was on its way up the lake to Kaslo for a ten-day maintenance layover. Many of the crew had left for holidays. Lily packed her bag with the contents of her stateroom locker and drawers. She said goodbye to the captain and staff who'd become good friends for almost three years.

This was more a formality than anything, because earlier the dining room staff had hosted a farewell party with the ship's cook, Sam Lee, providing a beautifully decorated cake. The captain had provided several bottles of champagne.

As Lily stepped onto the wharf in Nelson she thought about her parents on the ranch. She'd spent a week with the family telling them of her plans. She accepted that it was impossible for any of them to attend her wedding in Vancouver, where Jack, with the help of his sister, was making arrangements. She smiled to herself as she thought of her new life ahead. Tonight she'd be on the train, and, tomorrow, Jack would be waiting at the other end.

Following their September wedding at Christ Church on Burrard Street in Vancouver, with Jack's sister Grace standing beside Lily, and Jack's younger brother, Morris, as best man, they caught the CPR Ship Princess Maquinna for the overnight trip to Clayoquot. The ship travelled up the BC coast stopping every ten days at the fishing community.

The small community consisted of the police station/living quarters, a combined hotel store and a telegraph office. The total population was ten. The local people said to expect rain twenty days out of thirty. The rainwater was collected in barrels and used for all purposes.

When Jack and Lily arrived, a local youth carried their baggage to the house on the beach. Jack stopped short of the building he'd left two months before. It looked as derelict as he remembered, and a spasm of guilt passed over him to have brought his bride here. He took her hand and swallowed the distress.

"Looks like it needs lots of work," said Lily. She slipped off her shoes and kicked up the sand as she walked toward the ocean. Glancing back at Jack standing in front of the building that also housed the jail, she called out, "Forget the place for a minute, Jack. Come and join me. It's more romantic than any place I've ever seen."

Jack had made a small start on repairs on his earlier visit. He'd scraped the rust from the stove, covered the broken window with oilskin, and swept the floor clean. He'd made sure there were no bird nests in the chimney. Now, he collected small pieces of wood and got a fire going. "Tomorrow, I'll start on cutting a supply for winter," he said, "expect it gets pretty cold out here."

The bedroom held an iron metal bed, and in the closet a mattress had been well wrapped to withstand the elements. Jack hauled it out and placed it on the bed. The last occupant had covered a dresser with a tarp. "I'll give it a coat of paint," he told Lily. "For now, best leave our stuff in the suitcases."

"I'll warm up a pot of stew," she said, pulling a can from the box of supplies brought with them.

Jack left her to go to the rear of the small house to check out the jail. It consisted of two cells side by side, their doors open to reveal an empty pail in each. He'd been told there was no serious crime, and the jail was used only for the occasional prisoner who overindulged in alcohol. He secured the lock before entering the main house.

He rummaged in a box of household supplies and pulled out sheets and two quilts. "I'll make up the bed," he said.

"After we've eaten, let's go down to the beach for our coffee. I'll make a small fire. Might as well enjoy the best of the place."

For the rest of September and into the first week of October Lily and Jack got into the habit of taking their coffee to the beach after dinner. While she tidied up the kitchen, he would go ahead and get a fire started. He had made a seat of sorts out of a log for Lily to sit on. They would talk. One night she asked if he'd visited different places in England.

"A few, like I told you, I went several times to London with my buddies."

She snuggled up to him and pulled the blanket around them. "What did you do there?"

"First few times saw the sights, you know Buckingham Palace, that sort of thing, most of the time was spent in a pub."

"Did you like England?" she asked, a touch of homesickness catching her voice.

He added a chunk of wood to the fire. "It was all right. But I won't be going back any time soon."

"Sounds like you weren't overly impressed," she changed the subject. "I told you about being in New Denver while I waited for a ride to Kaslo. I went by your house and down to the lake and visualized you there as a child. Sounds like a happy childhood."

"It wasn't bad."

In the disappearing light, his expression sobered. He was remembering his brother so recently dead. He poked at the embers of the fire, scattering them. "I feel bad bringing you to this place, should have done better by you, Lily. My

Chief wasn't too happy either. He said that as soon as another post appears, I'll be first to get it."

"We're comfortable enough. I rather like the solitude."

"You do? That's good then."

Jack settled into the police routine, hiring a fish boat and crew to take him to the various outposts. It was only a matter of showing police protection. One day while repairing another leak on the roof, he saw a canoe pull a smaller one onto the beach. An Indian secured both crafts to a post and approached Jack, who'd walked down to meet him.

"Policeman, you need this," the native said, pointing to the smaller craft, a cedar dug out. "Waters as high as mountain." He raised his arms to the sky.

Jack had already met several natives of the area. "You make it?" He pointed.

"Me and my boy. He make many dug outs."

"Thank you," said Jack. "You want to meet my wife? Have a coffee?"

The man nodded and followed Jack to the house, where Lily, hearing the conversation came to the door. She had seen a few Indians in the store buying supplies, but she had never spoken to one. "Welcome," she said, and she moved aside to let him enter the house where he stood looking around.

She pointed to a chair at the table and turned to the stove to pour their coffees. He tipped the sugar from the bowl into the drink, disregarded the cream and took a big gulp, a smile appearing on his face.

Earlier that day she had made bread and cinnamon buns. She buttered a bun, set it on a plate, and passed it to the man. He eyed it for a moment before picking it up, then he bit into it. "Good," he said, and the same smile appeared on his face. Then, without a word, he jumped from the chair and headed for the door. "Policeman, use canoe. No become big fish."

The dugout saved Jack's life. Returning from a trip to Disappointment Inlet, in an area known as Graveyard of the Pacific, the sea turned mean, and Jack battled ten-foot waves. He had become skillful using the canoe, but what he faced was a different kettle of fish. He thought his luck had run out, and like the Indian said, he was about to become a big fish. He was not a praying man but with no sign of shore he did a good share of praying, and he did not give up. He paddled the canoe, riding it like a horse, right up onto the beach where Lily, wrapped in a blanket waited for him. She'd been there for hours. He'd rarely seen her cry, but this night she was sobbing. And later when they shared coffee with whiskey added, she told him she was expecting. "I thought I'd become a widow before becoming a mother," she said through her tears.

On a glorious fall day, more like summer, Jack suggested they go to a beach not too far from their own. But they'd have to go in the canoe. Jack raised on Slocan Lake was as happy on water as he was on the shore. "It's hardly any distance all," he assured Lily. "The change will do you good."

They spent a pleasant day in a grassy area near the beach returning to the canoe at sunset for the half hour paddle home. But they were in for a shock, had misjudged the tide, and were stranded. They pushed and dragged the canoe along the beach, Jack doing most of the work and finally reached open water where they discovered the canoe had sprung a leak.

"This is not supposed to happen," Jack said, venting his anger by kicking the canoe. "Stay here, Lily, there's sure to be something left by the tide that we can use to bail with. He strode down the beach and found several battered cans. Picking the best of them, he hurried back to Lily and got her settled in the canoe holding the cans. Vigorously, he paddled as Lily bailed the water settling in the bottom of the craft. It was very late when they beached the canoe and trudged to the house."

"Don't say a word," he said as he readied for bed. "Not one word."

The Indians in the area belonged to the Nootka tribe, and a few of them took a liking to the young policeman and his wife, especially after hearing about the welcome at the house. When they had potlatches, social events that later were banned by the government, they invited the couple to these. Here, the Indians gathered and exchanged their most prized possessions, and Lily often received a carving, woven basket, or a tray.

Jack also attended an occasional funeral, where the Indians hired professional mourners paid for their loudest and longest chant. Comforts of home such as photographs, and sewing machines were placed on the graves to speed the spirits on their way.

Spring arrived in Clayoquot, then, early summer. Just in time for the arrival of the baby, Jack received news he was to be transferred to Campbell River on Vancouver Island.

"I'd like you to go to Vancouver, Lily, to have the baby, stay with Grace. I'll come as soon as I can," he said. She took his advice and left while he remained in Clayoquot to finish up.

Jack promised Lily he would not go far in the canoe, use it only for fishing in the bay. He hired a fish boat and crew to make a last round of the territory, stopping to say goodbye to a few Indians he thought of as friends. Then he packed up their belongings and piled them into the wheelbarrow to take to the dock. He was leaving the small house in better shape than when he arrived. He wrapped the mattress well and left it on the metal bedstead.

He dragged the canoe up to the house and turning it upside down carefully propped it under the eaves as if he saying farewell to an old friend. Then he returned to the beach where he and Lily had sat so many evenings. It was within a day or two of a year since they'd arrived. He'd had a few bad scares on the water, but all in all, it had been a good year. He hoped that the new single man scheduled to arrive in a few weeks would fare as well.

When Lily arrived in Vancouver, heavy with child, she was met by Grace and her two boys. A week later in their home in Burnaby, attended by a doctor, Lily gave birth to a baby girl she named June.

The news came as Jack entered the general store with his wheelbarrow of household goods. He read the wire standing at the window looking out at the Maquinna being loaded. He smiled to himself. He was happy that they'd had a baby girl. The next one would be a boy.

As he travelled down the coast his thoughts moved from one thing to another—what it meant to be a father—for sure a better father than he'd had—and how Lily was adjusting well to being a policeman's wife. His thoughts then turned to his new post, what he'd encounter, his method of travel. He'd likely get a car since they were used more frequently. The transfer had not mentioned accommodation at Campbell River. People only talked about the number of salmon they caught, and size. But first things first. He was anxious to get his wife and baby settled in their new home. The visit with family would be brief.

As his intention, two days after arriving in Vancouver, he said, "Lily, my dear, say your goodbyes. We're leaving tomorrow at nine. I've booked us onto the ship that stops at Campbell River."

"Have we a house to go to?" she asked, as she moved the baby to her other breast to nurse.

"I expect so. I've wired ahead that we are arriving." But when they arrived, the family found the new detachment had no living quarters, no jail, not even a temporary lock-up. Prisoners were taken by motor launch to Quathiasky Cove.

For ten days they stayed at the Willows Hotel, then a suite came for rent above the general store. Jack worked from the kitchen table. But no car awaited.

This was remedied when he received a call to go to Nanaimo to pick up a model T Ford. Jack had never owned or operated a vehicle. After a half hour instruction, he left for home, desperately trying to stay on the road. "I took out a whole section of fence, didn't dare stop for fear of not getting going," he told Lily later. Operating the vehicle became a challenge. Almost every morning when Jack went to start it, one or more of the tires were flat.

The frequent trips by gas boat through Seymour Narrows were dangerous and a wildfire scare that shut down the only road, was another frightful experience. The family had made friends in and around the area and a couple from Courtenay invited Jack and Lily and baby for lunch, a two-hour drive from the police station. The day turned unusually warm, a dry heat that sucked the body's energy. "You could stay over," their friends offered.

"I don't like to leave the post unprotected," Jack said, "thanks, anyway. At least we have a reliable vehicle."

"Well, take a pail of water and a couple of towels to cool yourself off."

They were about an hour into the drive where the dirt road narrowed. Brush and small trees reached out almost touching the vehicle. Jack was familiar with this stretch of road from his patrols, and always took extra care driving through. He reached for the towel on the seat and mopped his face. "Sure, it is hot."

That's when he noticed the smoke. "Looks like a brush fire ahead, Lily. Roll up the window flaps and set baby down at your feet. I'm going to speed up a bit."

He drove a short distance then stopped. A smoldering bush had rolled onto the road in front of the car. Without a word, he reached into the back seat and pulled out two gray blankets and submerged them in the gallon of water. Then, leaving the vehicle, he walked around to Lily's side, and draped a sopping blanket across the car's hood and did the same on his side.

"Hold tight, my dear, I'm making a run for it," he said, as he climbed back into the car. In a matter of minutes, the brush fire was behind them. He pulled over to the side of the road, removed the ash covered blankets, and threw them into the back. Baby June was sleeping, a damp towel covering her.

At home, he parked the car. "I've got a question," said Lily. "How did you know you could make it through?"

"I know where the narrow section of the road ends, and with the gully ahead and only rocks, no trees, nothing to feed a fire. I'd never put you and the babe in danger, Lily. You should know that."

The unexpected was always happening, Lily decided. One day, when Jack walked in the door, she knew by his expression something drastic had happened. "I've lost the pup," he said, referring to their two-year-old spaniel. "She's gone into the gully with the car." He'd been out on a routine patrol and had decided to take the dog with him.

He told Lily the story. On a steep hill the brakes failed on the car. His only option was to ride it down the hill as it picked up speed and look for a place to jump out. As he headed into a curve, he pushed the door open and jumped. The car crashed through the underbrush and disappeared into the gully below.

"There's no way Roxy could survive," he said, shaking his head. "I hope she died instantly, not lying injured. Too late today to do anything, I'll get a team to pull the car out in the morning."

Early the next morning, Jack directed the teamster to where the car had disappeared, and he and his partner climbed down the steep gully to see what was involved to pull the vehicle out. Jack was standing by the horses when he heard a shout from the gully. "Looking for your dog, Constable?" The driver led a tail-wagging Roxy over the rocks. "Found her asleep in the backseat. She could do with a bowl of water."

In 1921, Lily and Jack and one year-old June were on the move again, this time to Vanderhoof in BC's Cariboo. Waiting for them was a twenty-year old three-room log house with a rough board floor full of splinters. The dark rooms had tiny sunless windows. Lily shook her head at the condition of the place and set to work to make the place livable.

A ten by twelve office with one steel cage for lock-up was attached to the rear of the house and all police business such a preparing court documents was transacted in this small area. Jack was given another Model T, in the same poor condition as the last. When stopping for any length of time in winter he had to drain the water and oil from the tank, reheat, then place both tanks back in the car. For breakdowns, he always carried a spare axle.

Other than the Hudson Bay fort at Fort St. James, there were no settlements in the area. Jack's police district extended twenty-five miles east, and sixty miles south to Tatuk Lake. To the north, bands of Indians lived in the Bear Lake country.

Because of the high prices received for furs, the Indians were encouraged to trap illegally. White fur buyers tried every means possible to get the pelts out of the province which charged a dollar royalty for each skin.

Many tricks were used, such as placing skins in the water tender on trains heading east, then removing them when across the border, or buying a passenger ticket for an eastern point and sending the furs through on a baggage ticket. This was frustrating for lawmakers.

The trappers in the north were courageous and suffered great hardship. In the winter evenings, with a warm fire crackling in the stove, and baby June tucked in her crib, Jack told Lily stories of the north, some from his own experience, others passed on to him. Joe Murray was one example of such courage. In the early 1900s, when he was a young man checking his trapline, he met up with a female grizzly bear with her cubs. Before the animal attacked, Joe shot and wounded her. But there was lots of life still in the creature. Before Joe knew what had happened his head was in the bear's mouth.

Joe's small dog distracted the bear, biting and worrying her, giving Joe the opportunity to crawl under logs and stay there until the animal left. But the bear had done its damage. Joe's eye was torn from its socket and hung from threads to his cheekbone. He knew if he was to live, he had to get back to his cabin. Crawling on hands and knees, passing out many times, he made it back to his cabin. To stop blood poisoning, he poured peroxide, the only substance available, into his eye. But he needed help.

Mrs. Lamont, an old timer in the Vanderhoof area, heard a commotion at her door, where upon opening it discovered Joe in poor condition. She dragged him to a chair in the house, and said, "You have two choices, Joe, wait until tomorrow for the train to Prince George, or let me sew the eye back in. If I do this, you must promise to get treatment as soon as you can."

Joe agreed to let her work on the eye immediately. She handed him a bottle of overproof rum to drink and deaden the pain while she worked. With the light of a coal oil lamp, using a darning needle with linen thread, she sewed the eye back in place and put a patch over it. After several days rest Joe returned to the trapline, and he did not go into Prince George for further treatment. Later, he tracked the bear down and shot it.

Lily was horrified at the story. Although she'd never met Joe Murray—long dead—she heard the story again and again from old Mrs. Lamont.

Lily came to terms with Jack's work, but she never stopped worrying. Part of his job was to handle disturbed people. One day he set out with a hired team and driver to investigate a complaint that a farmer was threatening his neighbors with a high-powered rifle. When Jack reached the shack where the man lived, snow was falling heavily, and darkness had set in. He knocked at the door and received no answer. Putting his ear to the door he heard movement inside.

He'd come prepared with a rail from the jack pine fence to break the door down, but a good shove opened the door. He leaped into the room, grabbed the rifle on the table, threw it into the snow and jumped the man who strangely enough was gentle and bewildered, and was arrested with no trouble.

"All part of the job, Lily," Jack said when he returned home.

She shook her head. Vanderhoof had different demands than Clayoquot or Campbell River.

Christmas Eve morning, Jack said court had been moved up, and he had to be there for his prisoner, Leon, a member of a known Indian family. "He's pleading guilty to assault," he said, "and he will be returning with me to serve his sentence. We'll be back in good time."

But the car as usual was unreliable and a wheel bearing had burned out. Jack saw the repairs were going to take some time so, he said, "Go on home, Leon. I'll pick you up in a couple of hours." Two hours later Jack went to Leon's house on the reservation. Leon's wife came to the door.

"He not home, not see him," she said, blocking the entrance with her body.

Jack peered over her head, saw the room was filled with Indians. "I'll return another time," he said, and he backed up.

Ten miles out on the road, the car broke down completely, and no amount of effort got it going. Still miles from home, Jack left his pack in the vehicle, and with a few essentials, he walked for three hours until he spotted a roadhouse where he could stay the night.

Earlier, while everything was happening to Jack, Lily was preparing a special Christmas Eve supper for when he got home. She was used to him attending court but they both hoped he would not have to do this until after the holiday. After she finished dinner preparations—a casserole of sweet potatoes and sausage—Jack's favorite—she changed June's diaper and placed her in a play area.

Then pulling the old sewing machine from under the bed, she continued working on flannel nighties for the child who had gone from crawling to taking a few steps. They had lunch, then it was June's naptime. Lily spent this free time reading or needlework. This day she had saved her mother's last letter to read.

Elizabeth wrote as regular as clockwork, and Lily did the same. She had not seen her mother for three years, and missed her, hoping that one day they'd live close enough for frequent visits. Her father was about the same, had acquired a third dog, another mixed breed. According to her mother, Will was happy enough, and still went into town every so often. Freddy and Ellen had married, and a year later, Ellen miscarried.

When four o'clock came Lily stoked up the fire for their dinner. June was back in the play area. Lily cut green beans to go with the casserole and set them in a pan of cold water. Five o'clock came with no sign of Jack. This wasn't unusual; he often was delayed. She mashed up sweet potato and a spoonful of sausage for June's dinner.

Holding back on cooking the beans, Lily let the fire die down, setting their meal back on the stove to keep warm. When six o'clock came and no sign of Jack, she looked out on the path and saw it had started to snow and was relieved with a reason he was late. No doubt the car was stuck. She bathed June and put her to bed in the crib that they had ordered from Eaton's. At ten o'clock she built up the fire for the night and went to bed.

The house was cold when she woke at six. Changing June's diaper and covering her well, she started the kitchen stove, saw the wood box was still half full. She was at a loss to know what to do. For Christmas Day, they'd planned to roast a duck for dinner served with regular potatoes. It was in the cooler on the porch ready for the oven along with the uneaten casserole. On the kitchen counter sat the wrapped pudding her mother had sent.

She pulled out the sewing machine and finished the nighties, hemming the extra cloth for dish towels. She warmed up soup for lunch and played with June. She felt at loose ends, didn't know what to do with herself. She wondered where she could go for help if Jack didn't return. The firewood needed replenishing. She bundled up and had the door open when she saw what looked like a snowman shuffling down the path. "Jack! You're a sight to behold." She hugged him through the layers of his clothing.

She pulled him into the house, where he shrugged off his jacket and dropped the beaver hat to the floor. He was exhausted. He sat for a minute at the table, then went to the cupboard above the sink and brought down a bottle of brandy and two glasses. "I know you're not much of a drinker, Lily, but today calls for one." He downed his in one gulp and half-filled the glass again. "I'm so sorry you've been worried. It all started with the damned car!"

While Jack stretched out on the couch playing with June, he told her what had happened.

"Do you think Leon will come in on this own?" she asked.

"I doubt it. He'll find some place to hole up for the winter," he placed his glass down. "What's for supper?"

"I don't feel like cooking the duck, I'll warm up last night's casserole. Stay where you are, I'll bring in the wood I was going for earlier," she joined him on the couch. "Merry Christmas. I wonder how many we'll have in this place."

Jack wrote up his report for the South Fort George office, and to his surprise found he'd been suspended without pay for two months due to losing a prisoner. He later heard he was the first constable to be affected by the new regulation. He hated telling Lily the news, money was not growing on trees. She said, not to worry, she still had a little put away for a rainy day. "Maybe not rain but snow," she said with a small smile.

"It was smart on your part not to try and arrest Leon," a friend told him later. "He was waiting for you upstairs in the house with a rifle." Through the winter Jack tried to arrest Leon, but he always had a pack of dogs warning him when Jack arrived.

The Fort St. James' Indians were in most part law abiding. They had not wanted this conflict with the police involving one of their own. The saga between Jack and Leon was not over. It was late spring, and the car was running again without a hitch. Jack had suggested Lily and the baby accompany him on a short patrol. They were a mile or so from the house when they saw a team approach with two Indians.

"I think we should ignore them," said Lily, "don't turn around. It looks like they're heading for the lock-up."

The team passed without incident. When the family got home, Leon was sitting on the front step. He looked up, a strange expression on his face. "All winter I be haunted," a hand on my shoulder, trapping no good. "My brother bring me, tell me to give myself up." Leon was sentenced to six months in jail.

Jack and his small family spent three years in Vanderhoof. In June 1924, he was transferred to Stewart, a mining town at the head of the Portland Canal amidst majestic snow-capped mountains. The district, two miles from Hider, Alaska, was small, and included the mining camps in the area. Their living quarters were poorer than the last one. The former constable had lived elsewhere, leaving the house neglected.

Jack took no responsibility for the bootlegging in full swing when he arrived. It operated from a dozen frame buildings lining the road to the dock and convictions were rare.

High stake poker games ran all night. The red-light district, a long row of houses that faced the tide flats, was considered one of the largest in Canada. The girls caused no trouble and mixed freely with the town. When Jack first arrived, he wondered how Lily would handle this environment, but she had learned to be tolerant of circumstances she knew nothing about. She always nodded pleasantly when passing any of the fancy women in town.

The liquor store, outlet for both Canadian and Alaska territory, did a steady business, with the girls from the 'line' their best customers. The girls mostly from American cities, were often products of broken marriages, sometimes supporting children left behind in places like Denver and Chicago.

Like any job, it had its occasional humorous side. Jack received a call to go to the Salmon River Glacier area to investigate a complaint that a supposedly deranged miner was sleeping with sticks of dynamite under his pillow at night. He persuaded the man to accompany him back to Stewart. The trip involved passing over numerous four-five feet crevasses. The man, an athletic Norwegian, well over six feet, leaped the chasms with great ease enjoying the challenge. Jack took the long way around, sometimes detouring more than a mile. The man was always waiting for him.

Lily found living in Stewart an interesting experience, but when Jack's transfer to Bella Coola came in 1925, she was pleased. She had worried when Jack left for his patrols in Stewart, never knowing what might happen. Besides a coastal area would bring better weather.

There was one small problem, however. She was eight months pregnant when Jack received the news of the transfer. After much discussion they decided to rent an apartment in Vancouver two weeks before the baby was due. If all went well, after her stay in the hospital, they would travel up the coast to their new home. Jack was scheduled to arrive in August.

But life doesn't always deal the cards that we wish. The delivery was easy enough, a nine-pound boy. Unfortunately, the baby they called John, was born with a condition called spina bifida. There was no cure. He would live a week or two. "I think you and June should go on ahead of me," Lily said. "I must stay here until…" her voice faltered… "until it happens. Grace said she'd help with arrangements."

Jack didn't want to leave Lily, but she insisted. After a six-day stay in hospital, she moved back to the apartment. She declined Grace's offer to stay there, wanting to be close for the baby's last days. Over a cup of coffee in the hospital cafeteria, the doctor who joined her said the baby was being made comfortable. Ten days passed.

"Mrs. Williams, how are you holding up?" The doctor slipped into a chair across from her.

"As well as to be expected," Lily said.

"I've been wanting to ask you, without being impertinent, how you acquired the burns on your neck and lower face?"

"In a fire when I was five years old," Lily said, in a matter-of-fact way.

"What kind of treatment did you receive?"

"Mostly ointments and massage, that's about it."

"I'm not an expert on corrective surgery, leave that to the specialists, but I have done minor repair. It consists of tiny snips that allows the skin to relax. Would you be interested in me having a look at what can be done? I would do the surgery in my clinic."

Lily glanced at her watch. She had taken the doctor and nurses' advice not to see the baby, after the first time, because of the distress. But each day she went to the maternity floor to glance through the glass at the healthy infants waiting to go home.

She turned back to the doctor. "I don't suppose it will do any harm. But it must wait until after the baby has gone." She stared hard at the doctor. "When do you think that will be?"

He fought back his emotions. "It's been longer because he's a strong little fellow…another day or two at the most." He pushed back his chair. "I'm so sorry, Mrs. Williams, so sorry."

Baby John died the next evening at thirteen days old. Grace made all the funeral arrangements. After they left the cemetery, she said, "When do you leave?"

Lily told her about the appointment with the doctor. "I don't know what he can do, but there's nothing to lose. I have the apartment until the end of the month, then I must go home. Jack and June have been on their own long enough."

The doctor's appointment was on a Monday. After he examined Lily at his clinic, he said, "There is not a lot I can do about the scars on your neck, but I can improve the area on the lower lip. What do you think?"

"I'm willing to see what you can do," she said. Lily returned to his office two days later. After a freezing solution was applied to her lip and surrounding area, Lily swallowed a sedative. A few snips and stitches, a swabbing, the procedure was over.

The doctor held a mirror to her face. "This is what I have done. You look like you've been in a war, by the weekend you'll notice an improvement."

Lily held off reserving her passage and stayed in the apartment until the lease expired. She returned once to the doctor's office and was reassured all was well. She met Grace several times for lunch, but most of the time she stayed quietly in the apartment or took lone walks where she could mourn her baby alone.

By the time she boarded the ship for the overnight trip to Bella Coola she was more like herself. She applied the medicated cream the doctor had given her, and a little make-up and gradually saw the improvement he had promised.

Lily hurried down the gang plank to Jack and June waiting on the wharf. June was bouncing up and down like a rubber ball. They were both smiling. She stepped forward into Jack's waiting arms, felt a relief at being near him. He swung her around to kiss her, then frowned. "Have you cut yourself?"

She touched her lip, "I'm sorry, of course, you didn't know I've had my lip looked at by a doctor. It's not finished healing."

"Oh!" He leaned over and gave her a peck on the cheek. They moved back to let handlers reload the ship and started toward the road. "Momma, Momma, hold my hand." June was jabbering away like a monkey as they walked home.

Lily had no idea what to expect for a house and was pleasantly surprised the post offered a neat four room wood frame house with a porch and back garden. More surprising was a telephone attached to the wall by the front door. "My goodness, you'll have to teach me how to use it," she said.

"It's easy, Momma. When it rings three times we answer."

June had gone to bed in a room that adjoined theirs when Jack poured two brandies and led Lily to the couch. "You've had a bad time and were very brave to stay alone in the apartment and wait it out. I still can't believe we lost him. When I looked at him the one time, he seemed perfect, but, of course, I couldn't see the space in his back. I wonder why that happened."

She sipped the brandy. "I suppose we'll never know. The doctor said it happens from time to time, something to do with the spine. You told June?"

"I told her the baby had gone to heaven."

She changed the subject. "Now, that I'm home you can get on with your work. How large is the area you cover?"

He sat back, relaxed, "It covers close to 100 miles, home of the Stick Indians. Seems, I'm also fire and game warden, and have to register vehicle licenses and vital statistics."

"My goodness, they're getting a pound of flesh."

He chuckled at her English saying. "That's not all, Lily. I have to enforce the Indian Act, particularly liquor infractions."

They sat quietly, Jack's arm around her shoulders. He still hadn't kissed her, likely turned off by her lip so raw. She set down her empty glass. "Guess it's bedtime."

The next morning June watched her mother package up the baby clothes, including a beautiful layette. It had been a surprising gift from a girl from the 'line'. A few days before leaving Stewart, there was a knock on the door. A neatly dressed woman stood on the step. "This is for your baby," she said, shyly. "We picked yellow not knowing if you were having a boy or girl." She turned to leave.

"This is very kind of you," said Lily. "Thank you and please thank the others."

She set the layette back in the drawer, picked up the package of clothing. "June, let's walk over to the clinic. I'm sure they know someone who can use these."

Throughout the years in various locations, Jack became comfortable with Indian ways, and Chinook, a trade dialect used by the Hudson Bay Company. Often one or two Indians would arrive at the family door, visit, have something to eat, then silently go on their way. They were usually dressed in buckskins. This is when the dialect was most useful.

Jack settled into the routine of his work, and Lily made a few friends in town. She was still surprised when the telephone on the wall rang, often with June running to answer on the third ring.

On the day the event happened, Lily baked bread. Experience prevented letting June near the stove, but she let her pound and roll the dough that included a few miniature buns. They were finished and the bread was covered with a cloth and set to rise.

Jack was still at home, working at a desk in his office when the phone rang. A local Indian, Peter Whitewash, armed with a 30-30 Winchester was threatening employees of the BC Packers Cannery. "I'll see if I can locate him," Jack said. He slipped on his uniform jacket, grabbed his revolver from the top of the file case and hurried out the door. He returned without locating the man.

He had lunch and was about to start writing up a report when the phone rang again. Peter had been seen again, still armed, heading for his home on the reservation.

Before going onto the reserve, Jack contacted three men, Milo, Jurgen, and Joe Saunders, a young Indian. Police procedure, before entering the reservation, required Jack to have at least one of these men with him. They stood a distance away when he approached the two-story house and knocked. When he got no answer, he backed up, at the same time looked at the upstairs window where Peter had lifted out the glass and stood muttering.

"Come on down," Jack shouted. "There'll be no trouble."

Jurgen hurried to the back of the house to watch if Peter tried to slip away. Jack shone his flashlight on the upstairs window, Milo beside him.

Suddenly, Milo said, "Watch out, Jack!"

The warning came too late. Muttering a few words, "I fix you, policeman," Peter fired.

The bullet hit Jack's hand that held the flashlight, like a slipped knife gutting a fish. Pieces of metal flew into his face as he fell to the ground and crawled away. He felt nothing as Milo lifted him up and was semiconscious as the men half-carried him to the Bella Coola Hospital where he was treated for a bullet that had ripped through his hand, travelled up his arm and exited at the elbow.

Meanwhile, Lily heard the telephone ring several times, but she didn't answer, then, something told her to pick up the receiver. "The policeman's been shot on the reserve," she heard, as a person passed on news. She sank to the floor in shock. She had always feared this would happen.

Fortunately, a second call from a nurse came quickly. "Lily, I'm calling from the hospital. We've got Jack here—he's okay. We're treating him for gunshot to his hand."

"I'll come right away."

"No, wait until morning when it's light. It's too risky for you to come now."

The following morning at daybreak, with June tightly holding her hand, Lily walked to the hospital, staying well below the grizzlies feeding on the upper slope.

"I'm buggered up," said Jack who was lying on a hospital bed his arm in a sling.

"Guess it could be worse," she said, a catch in her voice.

Peter Whitewash was persuaded by his mother to give himself up. While waiting to be transferred, Lily had the opportunity to meet Peter. "Why did you shoot my husband?" she asked.

"He my friend," said Peter, shaking his head, "Me have too much whiskey." He was charged with attempted murder but convicted of a lesser charge.

Jack was back home but only briefly. With Lily doing most of the packing, they were on the move again, going to Vancouver where Jack could receive more skillful medical attention.

They spent the winter in Vancouver in an apartment near the hospital where Jack spent a good part of each day receiving treatment. Slowly his hand and arm healed, leaving small bits of metal under the skin from the shattered flashlight. These stayed for the rest of his life as a reminder of what might have been. When his treatment was almost complete, his superintendent asked Jack to take on the Bowen Island detachment until something more permanent came along.

Moving to Bowen Island in the late spring of 1925 was like a holiday for the family. They stored their belongings in Vancouver, surprised at how much they'd accumulated. They purchased bathing suits at the Hudson's Bay on Granville—a cute polka dot outfit for June, a more subdued suit in green for Lily, and black trunks for Jack. At a sporting goods store, they bought an inner tube and life jacket to keep June safe. Having grown up on Slocan Lake in the Kootenays, Jack was comfortable around water. Lily was not. She still remembered bailing the canoe in Clayoquot, and how frightened she'd been.

Bowen Island was a perfect post for Jack whose arm was still far from normal. There was no crime on the Island. He investigated an accidental shooting which amounted to nothing. Another time he searched for three horses that disappeared through a broken fence, found them grazing a mile from the property. The worse incident was a capsized boat, but the owner managed to swim to shore.

The family spent most summer afternoons at the beach. They carried a cold dinner in a wicker basket along with blankets to a beach ten minutes away. Under the watchful eyes of her mother, June learned to paddle.

By the end of September days began to cool making beach trips less frequent. Jack started lighting the fireplace in the afternoons. Lily sensed he was getting restless. At the end of October, he received a wire from his chief to say the constable at Lillooet planned to retire. The post would be available if Jack wanted it.

"Yes," he answered immediately.

Lily had no idea where Lillooet was situated. She pulled out a BC map, and found the community alongside the Fraser River, at the start of the Cariboo Highway that had been a wagon road to the Goldrush in 1860.

Like other places they had lived, it was rich in native history, members of the Salish people. "Looks like a good place," said Jack, tracing his finger on the map. "I wonder how we get there."

They left Bowen Island early November, collected their stored items in Vancouver, and climbed aboard the Pacific Great Railway, known as the PGR. The weather in Vancouver had been rainy and miserable, but as the train chugged along the winding Fraser River, occasionally stopping at small communities, temperatures dropped and outside the land appeared to be bone dry.

It was late evening when the train stopped at the small station. Lily, Jack, and June climbed down, and an Indian family hopped on. Not knowing what to expect, the family were pleasantly surprised to find a reasonably sized house in neat condition with neighbors close by. They settled in and swiftly became part of the town. For the first time, June made a best friend, and in January, the two started grade one together. Only a few houses apart, Yvonne and June became inseparable. Because of the children, Lily, and Yvonne's mother, Mary, also became best friends.

With work and community activities that now included June's schooling, Jack and Lily rarely had any free time to sit down and talk. But one evening in the spring of 1926, a letter from Elizabeth, Lily's mother, forced the issue. Lily caught Jack as he was leaving the house for a meeting with the Fire Chief.

"Could you spare me a minute?"

"Of course."

"I've had a letter from Momma, mostly about Dad. He's not doing very well. I think I should go home; letters are not the same as being face to face." When Jack didn't say anything, she said, "I've talked to Mary, and she offered to have June come home with Yvonne after school and stay until you pick her up."

"Of course, you must go home. When do you want to leave?"

"After the meeting with June's teacher. I'll go next week, stay at the most ten days. Are you all right with this?"

"Lily, I'm all right with anything you want to do."

"I'll use my own money for the ticket."

"You'll do no such thing. You tell me your rail schedule and I'll take care of the tickets."

With the many moves, on the British Columbia coast and far north, Lily had not seen her parents or her brother for four years. She wired her mother that she was coming and asked her to arrange a ride with Little Joe. Her stay in Nelson was brief, only long enough to telephone Edith to say hello. Joe, who was starting to show his age, dropped her off at the ferry slip for a walk on, and she hiked up the hill to the ranch, out of breath when she got there.

Four years had changed her parents immensely, leaving her plenty of guilt that she had not found a way to visit sooner. Her mother was sixty-five years old, but she looked ten years older. Lily remembered her mother as a vibrant woman. But establishing a new life in Canada at middle age had changed her.

And her father, never robust, seemed to have shrunk in size and lost inches in height. As she sat across from them at supper, it was like looking at two old people. But it was obvious there was no change in the affection between them.

Over the next ten days, Lily accepted the difference in her parents. One evening toward the end of the visit, her mother said, "I notice your lip is much improved. The treatment was worth your while. I'm glad you had it done. Your accident will stay with me for the rest of my life."

She put a fresh cup of tea before Lily. "Losing the baby was dreadful for you. I wish I'd been there to help. Will you try again?"

Looking thoughtful, Lily said, "I don't know, Momma. I'm thirty, I suppose there is still time. We haven't talked about it. I think we're afraid it could happen again."

"Not too likely," Elizabeth said, changing the subject. "Do you see a difference in your father?"

Lily avoided answering directly. "I notice you do most of the chores, that's hard on you."

"Oh, I get help, Freddy comes by twice a week, and I still call on a boy from the store. I manage."

Spontaneously, Lily leaned over and kissed her mother. "I may not visit often, but I think about you every day,

Momma. And I tell June all the little stories you told me, so that one day she can pass them on."

"That's good." Elizabeth glanced at the tiny gold watch always pinned to her dress. "Time to feed the dogs and chickens. They don't like waiting. Your dad is sitting out back in his usual chair. While I'm busy would you keep him company?"

"I'll make a fresh cup of coffee and take it out to him. Has he seen a doctor lately?"

Elizabeth was mixing up a bowl of leftovers for the dogs. "A doctor from Nelson comes once a month and sets up back of the store. I make sure your dad sees him."

"That's good. What does the doctor say?"

"Not too much. The one time we talked, he said your dad had a bad heart. He prescribed pills to be taken twice a day."

"I suppose that's all that can be done." Lily washed their teacups at the sink and put the kettle on to boil. "You go on with your chores, Momma. I'll look after dad."

Two days later, she waited at the ferry slip with her mother by her side. Without talking they watched the ferry leave from the other side of the bay. "You'll phone if there's any change with dad?" Lily said as the ferry approached the wharf.

"Of course. I use the phone at the store. I thought about getting one in the house but changed my mind."

The ferry tied up, and a car drove off, followed by a few foot passengers. Lily reached out and embraced her mother. "Goodbye, Momma, it's been lovely visiting you. Don't you overdo it. I'll write as soon as I'm home."

Elizabeth set her mouth firmly to stop the quiver. "Give my love to your darling daughter, and that good looking husband of yours."

The ferry turned into the channel, and Elizabeth was hidden from view.

After her visit home, Lily thought constantly of her father. This made her more observant of Jack's health. When they met ten years ago, he smoked a half package of cigarettes a day, now he was up to over a package. Her father had never smoked—as captain of the rugby team he frowned against it. But her uncles all smoked cigars.

When Jack's smoking habit increased, especially after the gunshot, she commented on it. "It's not good for your lungs," she told him, but he laughed this off, and teased her by offering a cigarette.

"Not on your life," she said pushing his hand away. She rationalized that at least he wasn't a drinker.

1926 ended with a flurry of activity—Christmas parties, school concerts, and then the New Year's Ball. Lily ordered an elegant gown from a shop in Nelson and bought long black gloves locally. When Jack was checking his wardrobe, she suggested he splurge on a new suit. He mainly was in uniform but there were times when he needed regular dress clothes.

They were sipping a brandy before going to the ball when Lily said, "Do you realize we've been here longer than any place? Perhaps, headquarters has forgotten us. Let's hope they continue to do so. I don't worry nearly as much as I used to when you're out on the job."

He reached down and took her hand. "Do you want me to dig up a bit of excitement? Maybe a shooting or a stabbing. How about a murder or two? Wouldn't want you to forget how to worry about me."

She slapped his hand.

Playfully, he said, "Careful. You'll damage my good arm."

In late July, her father died in his sleep, not the kind of excitement that Lily wanted. Freddy telephoned with the news. Elizabeth followed up with a call a day later. She said she was all right, but Lily wondered. Despite her assurances, Lily didn't think her mother would ever be the same now that her beloved Will was gone.

"No need to come home," Elizabeth said. "Your father was not a churchgoer, there'll be no official service. Next time you are in Nelson, we'll go together to the cemetery. But I have been thinking it's time to meet my granddaughter. I'll visit in the fall."

When June heard her grandmother, Elizabeth, was coming she danced around the room. "Where is she going to sleep, Momma? She can have my room."

"Thank you, my dear. You won't have to move out of your room, I'm going to put Grandma in the sewing room. It's small but gets lots of light from the window." The room was used more for a variety of purposes that included sewing. They got to work with a borrowed ¾ size bed from Mary, and an easy chair moved out of the living room. By the time they were finished the room had a warm, comfy look to it.

Grandma Elizabeth settled in for a month visit with hardly a moment to herself. June tagged after her like a puppy dog. Elizabeth didn't tell the family her plans right away. Then one evening at supper she said, "I'm selling the ranch."

Lily looked up from eating her dinner. "I'm not surprised. Will you stay in Taghum?"

"I won't sell until the spring when I settle the dogs in new homes. Whoever buys the ranch will likely want the chickens." She picked up her fork and continued eating her dinner.

"And then?" asked Lily.

"Freddy and Ellen have asked me to live with them. I should get a decent price for the property, will be able to pay my way…wouldn't have it any other way."

"Would you consider going back to England?"

Elizabeth dropped her knife with a clatter. "What a thing to say. Why would I ever do that? There's nothing there for me. My home is in this country. My family is here, and Will not too far way." A tear slid down her cheek.

When it came time to return home, Elizabeth was packing her few belongings, Lily standing in the doorway, June trying to help. "I don't suppose you'd like one of the dogs?" she suddenly said. "Old Gyp hasn't much time left, and Penny about the same. I call her a bad Penny because she always gets into mischief. But the Belgian Sheepdog is a beauty, and she's only two years old."

"What's her name?" asked June, dropping a blouse she was trying to stuff into the suitcase.

"Will named her Black Betty." Her eyes misted over.

Lily paused, "I don't know, Momma, we're sure to move before long. I'll have to ask Jack."

"Let me know. I'm not going anywhere until the spring."

When Lily approached Jack that evening, he said, "Moving with a dog is difficult."

"Momma has never asked anything of us," said Lily. "It's Freddy and Ellen who help Momma out, not us. Besides, a pet is good for a child."

He patted her on the shoulder. "I'll think about it." He did not mention it again.

Elizabeth sold the ranch, and Penny, who survived Gyp, stayed with the new owners. Black Betty moved with Elizabeth to Freddy and Ellen's house in Nelson.

Then in the summer of 1928, while picking blackberries on the slope above the house, Elizabeth had a small stroke. She returned home after spending two nights in the Nelson hospital. In the fall of that year, Jack was transferred to Vernon.

"We'll be there only a short while then, I'm taking over the Chase detachment."

"This is the best news I've heard in a long time," Lily said. "I'll be closer to my family."

Family, thought Jack. He'd not seen any of his since recovering from the gun shot. But he didn't make an issue of this, just suggesting that they begin to pack.

He carried out his duties in Vernon from the office with a secretary to answer the phone. One day she received a call that a rancher had not been seen for some time. She turned to Jack, and said, "The old fellow lives on a two-bit place in the hills. Sounds like you should take a look."

He was glad to get out of the office for a change. "Wear your high boots," the secretary advised. "You could run into rattle snakes."

Rattle snakes? He'd met up with grizzlies in Bella Coola. Wolves and the occasional cougar in Vanderhoof. Plenty of coyotes in Lillooet, but never a snake. Pulling a face, he yanked his high boots from his locker.

Jack found the dirt road to the ranch, a broken-down location that had not seen a working hand for many days, if ever. He saw no snakes, rattlers or otherwise. The front door to the cabin with missing steps, was partly open. He stepped into what appeared to be a living room, kitchen combined with a room off it. The old rancher was half on and half off the bed, obviously long dead.

Jack stood for a moment taking it all in, the pail by the bed, the smell of death making him gag. Then a small movement alerted him. Curled around the rancher's foot was a large snake, and several smaller ones, likely newborns. The intrusion woke Mama, and she uncoiled and raised her head as if to protect her young.

Jack stepped back, tripping over an upturned bucket. Mama Rattler slithered toward him, and he heard her distinctive rattle. He wasted no time in getting out of the house and down the path to the car where he sat for five minutes breathing in cool air from the blower.

Back at the office he said to the secretary, "You were right. There are snakes out there." Then, he said, "I don't know who brings a body out under those conditions but please call them. On your life, I'm not going back there."

At home he told Lily about the incident. "Funny thing, I'd rather meet up with a wolf or coyote than a rattler. I don't mind admitting that it shook me up."

While living in Vernon Lily managed several visits with her mother and Ellen. Freddy was usually at work. Lily also renewed her friendship with Edith who had separated from George.

Jack received his transfer to Chase in 1929, and Lily went to Nelson to tell her mother the news. "We have a good-sized place, Momma, and a fenced back yard. I'm willing to take Black Betty home with me."

"What will Jack say?" Her mother's eyes were sparkling.

"He once said whatever I did was fine with him. I'll hold him to his word."

June changed schools again. Fortunately, she was a bright child, and a different school was not a problem. Jack's duties in Chase were the same as those in Vernon, except he did not have a secretary. With two fingers, he tapped out his reports on an old typewriter, and Lily answered the phone.

When she arrived home with Black Betty, Jack raised his eyebrows, but true to his word, he said nothing. He strengthened the fence with June giving advice. Black Betty soon became plain Betty. She never let June out of her sight.

Lily and June missed their Lillooet friends, but gradually they met other people and having a dog helped June adjust to a new home. This was their seventh move in nine years.

Lily saw the small health changes in her mother when she visited—walking slower, carefully rising from a chair and less appetite. Elizabeth was only sixty-eight years old, about the same age as Jack's mother now living in Vancouver in excellent health. Iris Williams had opened a tearoom on Seymour Street managing it entirely on her own. Lily wondered if the loss of her father had affected her mother's health. But when asked, Elizabeth said she was fine.

The ranching community of Chase was a quiet place to live, and there was no serious crime. A highlight of Lily's day was picking up the mail at the post office. She often lingered to have a cup of coffee with the postmistress. One day the woman said, "If you need someone to help with your housework, I know the right person." That's how Elvira MacPhee, shortened to Mac, became a part of the family.

In the summer of 1929, Freddy and Ellen brought Elizabeth to Chase for a holiday. Lily did not have to rearrange furniture to make room for her mother. The previous constable had three children, each with his own room. Freddy and Ellen stayed for tea, then left for the hotel in Vernon. Never in Lily's life had her mother slept past seven a.m., but she stayed in bed until Lily brought her a cup of tea well past eight. And by nine at night, she was in bed.

Lily was clearly worried, and when her brother and wife arrived back to drive Elizabeth home, she mentioned these changes.

"You're worrying over nothing," said Freddy. "It's a different routine, that's all. When I get mother home, she'll be as right as rain."

"I hope so."

A subdued Freddy phoned the first week of March the next year. Elizabeth had another stroke. This one more serious. She was in the Nelson hospital.

"Be honest, Freddy, should I come?"

He didn't answer at first, then he said, "I think you'd better come, Lily."

Elizabeth was unconscious when Lily and June arrived at the hospital a few days later. "I want to see Grandma," said June. "I don't care if she's sleeping."

"All right, just for a minute."

"Do you think she knows I'm here," said June, standing at the door.

"I'm sure she does. Now, quickly say goodbye, and I'll wait outside."

June tiptoed into the room. "Goodbye, Grandma. Thank you for giving me Black Betty. She's very happy and runs all over the yard and dad fixed the fence so she doesn't get out."

Elizabeth died two days later. Lily and Freddy arranged burial in the plot next to William and returned to the house where Ellen had tea waiting.

The following day, Lily said to Freddy, "June and I need to go home, she's missing far too much school. Thank you for giving Momma a good home. I'm sure the thrift shop will be pleased to have her clothing. All I would like is the wide silver bracelet and her watch she never was without. I'll give it to June when she's older."

"Don't become a stranger now that mother is gone," said Freddy.

"I won't let that happen; you and I are the only two left from the old days."

Elizabeth's death was hard on Lily. And it wasn't long before Jack noticed how quiet she had become. He wasn't sure how to approach this but needed to say something. He waited until they returned to the car after buying groceries in Vernon. "Let's get milkshakes and have them in the park before we go home," he suggested.

"All right," she said listlessly. They found a park bench and sat down.

"I want to talk to you about your mother's death," Jack said. "I know how you feel because I felt the same way after Bert died. It's a terrible feeling of loss to know you'll never see the person again."

"My mother was too young to die," she said. "I blame my father."

"Really? Why?"

"Because he caused Momma so much worry, and she worked so hard."

Jack took her hand. "It's obvious your father was your mother's whole world. Whatever she did for him, she wanted to. You have to get over this feeling of blame, get on with your life—our life."

"I'll try."

"What would you say we try for another baby? We're both young. Your mother would have been pleased."

"You're not afraid after what happened before?"

"I read up on it one day when it was quiet in the office. It's not likely to happen again." They drove home each in their own thoughts.

Jack's words stayed with Lily. When her spirits were down, she read one of her mother's old letters. Elizabeth had always been upbeat. There never was a sign of discontent about her life, quite the opposite.

Despite Jack's suggestion they try for another child, pregnancy didn't happen, so Lily put the thought aside. She joined a woman's group that met in the church hall, and she volunteered at June's school. Gradually, she felt like her usual self, until one morning following breakfast, she rushed to the bathroom to throw up. She sponged her face with cold water, pressed her hands to her stomach, and said aloud, "I don't believe it!"

Lily had no problems throughout the pregnancy, in fact, she felt more alive than for a long time. She arranged with the housekeeper, Mac, to stay at the house while she was in Vernon having the baby. When living there briefly, Lily had made a new friend, Elizabeth, who conveniently lived two blocks from the hospital. She invited Lily to stay while waiting for the baby to arrive.

In the middle of April, 1932, Jack drove Lily to Elizabeth's house. "Call when you go into the hospital," he said. "I'll come right away."

On the morning of the 21st, Lily said to Elizabeth "I'm feeling a few twinges. I'm going to walk down the hill to the hospital and admit myself." Later that afternoon, Lily gave birth to a nine and half pound baby girl. Jack was out on patrol and did not get to the hospital until late that night. They had already chosen a name if the baby was a girl. Elizabeth May after both grandparents.

"Oh, you named the baby after me," her friend said, "or is she named for the little English Princess?" Lily smiled and said nothing.

Five days later, Lily, Jack and June brought the baby home to Chase. Mac was at the house waiting, and from then on took over much of the care of the baby freeing Lily to help Jack with his office work.

Mainly due to Mac, the baby's name got shortened to Betty. Jack was laughing when he said, "We can't have two

Betty's," referring to Black Betty. "Let's call the dog Pup." So, the problem was solved.

Betty thrived under the attention of a household mainly of adults. This included the watchful eyes of Pup who followed the infant around as she started to crawl, then learned to walk.

In a rare free moment, Lily decided to bake. She set the ingredients for a cake on the kitchen counter. She added a stick of wood to the fire to bring it up to heat, checking the dial on the stove as it slowly rose. She kept an eye on Betty who'd toddled to the back of the room. Lily had spooned the batter into the pan when she heard the scream.

For a moment she didn't know where it came from? She looked this way and that—saw her precious baby trying to crawl from behind the hot water heater, her plump little body convulsing as she held a small arm high.

Jack, working in his office heard the screams and came running. He swept the babe from the floor, carried her to the sink and emerged her entire arm into cold water. Horrified, Lily watched as the water covered the burn that extended from her tiny finger past her wrist.

The cold water had effectively quietened the child's screams. She was as limp as a rag in Jack's arms. Lily's own accident came back as a relived nightmare. She slumped to the floor in a faint.

She came to with a wet cloth over her face. Jack was holding the baby, a towel wrapped around the tiny arm. "I have to take her into the hospital in Vernon," he said, as he helped Lily up. "Do you want to stay here or go with me?"

"I'm coming," Lily shook her head to rid it of the fog. "First, I need to call the school to tell June we'll be home as soon as we can." June, now thirteen, often stayed home on her own.

Twenty minutes later they were on the way. The baby, her arm wrapped in a towel, was whimpering as she lay across Lily's knee. And Lily's tears would not stop.

"Stop blaming yourself," Jack said. "You haven't got eyes in the back of your head." His reasonable tone strengthened her.

"I know, but she was perfect, now she has to live with this—I know what that is like."

The doctor who delivered Betty had moved his practice to Vancouver. A younger doctor gently carried the child into his examining room. He was murmuring to her, like a lullaby, and continued to while he checked the arm. He paused when he saw the scars on Lily's face.

"We've come a long way in treating burns. How long ago for you—twenty years?"

Lily touched her face. "Closer to twenty-five."

He spread a bit of medicated cream on the babe's arm, covering it with a thin gauze. He looked up, "Just leave the gauze on for a short while, to stop baby from touching. Then we want the air to do its magic. Could you bring her back in a week?"

Lily waited with Betty in reception while Jack returned to the examination room. "If I could have minute of your time, doctor? My wife is terribly upset. She may not be able to sleep."

The doctor wiped his hands on a towel. "I can understand why she's distressed having undergone a similar accident, although by far more serious." He shook a few tablets into an envelope and handed it to Jack. "This will help."

While driving home, Jack said, "Are you okay?"

"I'm all right. But I feel sad. The shape of the burn is so much like a bird's folded wing. The scar is going to stay, even if the doctor says otherwise. And it will always remind me the same way my accident reminded Momma."

June was anxiously waiting at home. After an explanation, Lily called Mac who had taken a few days off. "We need you," she said, her voice shaking.

Lily was getting ready for bed when Jack entered the room with a glass of water and a tablet. "The doctor said this will help you relax."

"I don't need any pills," she said brushing by him, hurrying down the hall to the babe's bedroom, where Mac resting on the couch, quickly got up.

"Don't you worry, Mrs. Lily, I'll take care of her. You go on to bed."

The next day Lily lifted the gauze from Betty's arm and applied the cream. As the days moved ahead, the arm healed. But the scar remained as Lily forecasted.

The months moved ahead, with rumor of another transfer. Before their lives became disrupted, Lily decided to have Betty baptized. It was not important to Jack, but he said to go ahead and make the arrangements. For God father, Lily chose Mac's brother, Herman, who was often at the house visiting his sister, and a new acquaintance, Ruby for God mother. The service was held in the small Anglican Church in Chase, with refreshments served afterwards by the church ladies. Lily felt she had done the right thing, even if Jack wasn't interested. It was only a short time later that he received his transfer to Revelstoke. June was fifteen and Betty was three.

The Revelstoke detachment did not supply housing for their police. Fortunately, there were places to rent. Several police officers worked out of the downtown location and along with providing police protection, the men often performed civic duties, such as a mounted police escort for the royal visit in 1937.

Another duty was protection for a Hollywood film crew who stayed several weeks in the area to film the movie Silent Barrier. June was chosen as one of the extras in the film. Many high-profile citizens, including the police and local dignitaries, received invitations to the various social events involving the movie.

Life was busy for the young constable and his family. Lily was happier in a way she'd never felt before, making new friends, joining other women in various groups, singing in the church choir. At times, she wondered if she was too happy, if this feeling of contentment wouldn't last. Even so, she wasn't prepared for what was about to happen She'd enrolled Betty in ballet classes and encouraged her to sing. Each year the dance school held a variety show in the town hall. When making up the program, the music teacher asked Lily for permission for Betty to be involved even though she wasn't yet four.

She held out the program she was working on, filling in names. "If you agree I'll place Betty second to last."

"She's a little young, don't you think?"

"Yes, but the audience will love her." Lily agreed.

The hall was packed and while Betty waited over an hour to perform, she sat squirming until she fell asleep.

Feeling the child leaning against her, Lily began to regret her decision to let her participate.

Finally, after a nod from the dance instructor, Lily took Betty into the dressing room, and helped her into a version of a Shirley temple outfit. Instead of a mass of Shirley Temple curls, Betty's hair hung in long golden ringlets. Lily left her at the entrance to the stage door and hurried back to her seat.

Betty danced onto the stage, twirled twice in her pink ballet shoes, stood tiptoes, relaxed, and began to sing the Good Ship Lolli Pop. Then with a final twirl she danced off the stage. The audience clapped loudly, many standing as they continued to clap. Lily hurried backstage, where she found Betty struggling to remove her dress.

"You carried that out perfectly, now let's find your dad and go home." It was well past nine o'clock.

Betty had climbed into her bed. "Momma, could I have some orange juice?" She drank a little, pushed the glass away, turned on her side and went to sleep. The next morning, she woke with a raspy throat. By afternoon she could barely speak. By evening she had a temperature of 104.

"Call the doctor, Jack, Betty's picked up a germ. I knew she shouldn't have performed in the concert."

"It may be the start of the measles, or one of the childhood diseases," the doctor said. "Give her lots of fluids, and aspirin. I'll come by tomorrow."

Betty lay in the bed, hardly moving. "It looks like strep throat," the doctor said on his return visit, shaking his head. He had examined Betty's glands and throat. Her temperature had dropped slightly.

She did not improve. Days went by with Betty taking only a little orange juice. Her body lost its chubby look. Her face thinned. Jack or Lily carried her to the bathroom taking turns to sit beside her bed, never leaving her alone. All the joy left the household. They spoke in whispers.

One day, several weeks into the illness when Jack was sitting by Betty's bed reading to her, he heard a strange gurgling sound coming from her throat. Without thinking he grabbed her and turned her upside down. A mass of thick yellow substance poured from her mouth. "Lily, come quick!" he shouted.

With Jack holding her over the bathtub, Lily cleaned Betty up, then set her against a pillow in her bed. "Call the doctor, Jack, please, to come right away."

The child was quietly sleeping when he arrived. "I've been doing some reading on Betty's condition," he said. "It's the strep throat family, called quinsy—very dangerous. It's a good thing someone was here, otherwise the child would have suffocated. It's like a boil bursting."

From that day on, Betty slowly recovered. She took a little milk and porridge, and soft bread. But it was well into the fall before she returned to her former self.

The dark cloud that had descended on the family continued, this time involving Jack. During spring break, Jack and a young man set out to take the mail by sleigh to the tug Beaton that was locked in by ice on the lake at Arrowhead. Ice breakers that normally kept the ice clear had not been able to get in for several days. When Jack and the youngster who occasionally helped on a patrol set out with the sleigh, the ice appeared stable, but then some of the sections broke away. "We'd better get back to shore," said Jack. But it was too late, they were trapped.

Jack felt responsible for the young man, who was no more than a boy, and now shaking with fear as well as the cold. They were standing on a floating chunk of ice that was rapidly moving away from the ship. "Hold tight," said Jack. "I'm going to signal the Beaton again. I don't think they're aware of our predicament. After several tries, Jack moving the flashlight back and forth, a crew member spotted the two precariously balanced on floating ice. With a return signal, they maneuvered the tug in closer, and began to throw out planks. Jack and the youngster slowly worked their way to the boards and after many mishaps, cold and wet, waited through the night to be rescued."

When Jack arrived home the next day, he did not tell Lily much about the ordeal. He did not tell her about donning dry clothes while his own hung on overhead racks. Or drinking hot rum by the potbellied stove, thinking he'd never felt so cold. Even years later he gave Lily a watered-down version of the night on the Arrowhead.

In early 1939, the papers were full of conditions in Europe. Jack came home one day to say there was talk of Britain entering a war with Germany. "It seems we've hardly got over the other one," he said, shaking his head.

"Thankfully, you're too old to be called up," said Lily. Jack was nearly forty-five.

"There's talk of me being transferred," he said, some weeks later. "I waited to hear definitely before telling you."

"Oh? And where might it be?"

"How would you like to live on the coast?"

Looking thoughtful, she said, "It would give June the opportunity to go to university. She's talked about that for years." June was nineteen, working in a drugstore in town.

"I'll let you know when I hear more," said Jack. A few weeks later, he said, "My transfer is confirmed. I'm joining the Burnaby detachment. Why don't I ask Grace to look around for a place we can rent?"

At the railway station, Betty clutching a coloring book, and June standing sedately, they said goodbye to their neighbors and boarded the train. A small house on 4th Avenue in Vancouver awaited them. After working briefly out of the Burnaby office, Jack informed Lily he was to be promoted to the plain clothes division and they would be moving again, this time to Vancouver's north shore.

Jack's work in North Vancouver involved national security for industries such as the Burrard Dry Dock. At the same time, he investigated major crime. He was on call 24 hours a day, and often worked half the night.

With June employed by the war department in Ottawa, the north shore home consisted of a family of three plus two dogs.

Betty, twelve years younger than her sister, was a student at the school across the street from the house. She had recovered well from her illness in Revelstoke but was prone to ear and throat infections and accidents. She'd pulled a planter over her chest trying to climb in a window; she'd gashed her leg climbing over a fence. The final straw was being hit by a lacrosse ball in the school parking lot. This required her to use crutches, her knee wrapped in an elastic bandage.

The war in Europe dragged on. For Jack, it meant long hours at work. For Lily, it was a matter of getting used to ration coupons and remembering to drop the backout curtains at night. She joined other women to help with the war effort, rolling bandages for the Red Cross. For children like Betty, it meant gas mask practice at school, collecting silver paper rolled into balls, working in their Victory Garden, and accepting six cent chocolate bars.

The war made Lily set aside any thought of seeking a professional opinion of the scars on her neck, chin, and lower lip, especially when seeing many discharged servicemen appear on Vancouver streets with terrible wounds, some missing an arm or leg, others covering their faces with scarves or bandages to hide their injuries.

It was a chance meeting with a young woman that prompted Lily into action. She was waiting for the streetcar in Lynn Valley after buying a few geraniums at the nursery. A woman struggling to hold two large shopping bags of plants, while trying to open her purse had her back to Lily.

"Can I give you a hand," said Lily, stepping forward.

Forced not to be rude, the woman who had a long scarf wrapped around her neck, turned. "Thanks. I can manage."

Never in all her life had Lily seen a person so badly scared. White lines crisscrossed the woman's face not covered by the scarf. Her nose was oddly flattened, and her eyes had a strange pulled, dead look.

The streetcar, preparing to stop, saved Lily from saying more. They both climbed in, the woman taking a seat near the back.

Lily hesitated, then she took the seat across from the woman as the trolley looped around and started its swaying journey into town, down the Grand Boulevard. "You must have a large garden," Lily said, pointing to the bags at the woman's feet. "Mine's mostly vegetables but I have a couple of planters that need filling."

The woman adjusted her scarf and nodded, clearly not wanting to talk.

"I'm not a curiosity seeker," said Lily, "but were you in fire? I know what that's like." She pointed to her own neck and chin. "I keep intending to see a doctor, find out if there's any new treatment available."

The woman uncovered part of her face, enough to talk. "The war is bringing new treatments called plastic surgery. You should ask about them." She reached into her purse and drew out a card. "You can have this. He's one of the best in the country." She glanced out the window, quickly pulled the cord to signal her stop, grabbed her two bags and hurried up the aisle to the middle exit. "I was pushed into a bonfire," she called out as she stepped down.

Lily did not phone the number on the card immediately. She told Jack about meeting the woman. "My scars are nothing compared to hers," she said. But in the fall of 1943, she called the number and made an appointment.

The doctor's office was situated in a medical building on Vancouver's Georgia Street. Lily stood outside the revolving door about to change her mind when someone impatiently pushed her into the foyer. Recovering her balance, she walked to the elevator and pushed the button.

The doctor's manner was reassuring as he waited for her to say why she had come. She told him about meeting the woman, about her own accident years ago, how she learned to live with her appearance.

"Have they prevented you from enjoying your life?" he asked, kindly.

Startled, she said, "Oh, no! I have a wonderful life, an interesting life. My husband's a police officer. I'm always meeting new people, lived in different places."

"And your husband? And your children? Would they be happier if you looked differently?"

"I doubt it. They know me as I am."

He sat for a moment without saying anything. "I'm sure you'd like an honest opinion," he finally said. "I'm familiar with the woman you met. Hers is an unusual case. I did what I could for her. She went through an immense lot of pain. Many people who come to me are unaware of the stress involved in corrective surgery. And there's no guarantee they will be happy with the results. If they insist on it, I go ahead, of course. I'd like you to go home and think this over carefully. In the short time we have talked, I see you as a well-adjusted, happy woman. If I were you, I'd leave everything as is."

Lily hadn't known what the doctor would say, but certainly it wasn't this. He smiled kindly and walked her to the door. He knew she would not be back. As Lily took the elevator to the lobby, she felt a sense of relief that she had put the matter to rest.

On an early evening, three days later, Lily and Jack were sitting on the veranda enjoying a cup of coffee. Across the street in the school parking lot, Betty and several friends were chatting. "So, what did the doctor say?" Jack asked. Involved on a case, there had been no opportunity to talk.

"He suggested I carry on enjoying my life," Lily leaned over and plucked a weed from the planter. "He didn't actually discourage the surgery but came close to it."

"Were you disappointed?"

"Not really. What's your opinion? You've never said."

"It isn't for me to decide. But I'm happy the way you are. Are you going back?"

She picked up his empty cup. "No. I'm done with the whole thing."

Betty had said goodbye to her friends. She hobbled across the street, using one crutch and joined her mother on the top step where she was now sitting.

Jack looked down at the two of them, slipped his arm over Lily's shoulder. "I didn't mention it before, but one of the guys from the office offered us his cottage on Bowen Island for a week or two. No charge. What do you say we take a holiday? I'm booked off for two weeks in July."

Lily plucked another weed from the planter. "It's unusual for you to suggest a holiday. Are you leading up to something? Like another move?"

"No, we're here for the duration of the war. I didn't want to interfere with what came from the doctor's appointment. Now I know you've settled your mind on that, I see no reason we can't have a vacation," he reached down and helped her from the step. "I'll call Dave right away."

"I'll write June," said Lily, as she pushed open the screen door.

For a moment, time stood still, then the telephone rang. Jack answered. He bolted up the stairs, reappeared, buckling on his gun belt, slipping his arms into the sleeves of his trench coat. The door banged shut behind him.

Betty dumped her homework bag on the kitchen table as she came in the house.

Lily pulled down the first of the blackout curtains. Life was back to normal. They moved into a new chapter of their lives.

Epilogue

Jack retired as a provincial police officer in 1950, receiving many commendations for outstanding police work during his career. Lily and Jack were married for 48 years before he died in 1967 at age 72 with end stage emphysema. They had lived in many towns in British Columbia but settled in Vancouver in later years. Lily had a good life, always supportive of family and friends, and died one day before her 99th birthday. She made multiple trips back to England including visits to her birthplace. Lily and Jack had seven grandchildren with daughters June and Betty. She is also well remembered by most of her 13 great-grandchildren.